DAYBREAK

INTERNATIONAL BESTELLING AUTHOR
TK LAWYER

Dedication

For my amazing American Foxhound, Molly- the inspiration for Weldon's shadow side.

I love you, my furry friend. Jim and I thank you for being a beautiful part of our lives.

Chapter One

Weldon grabbed ahold of her hips as she slid from his grasp.

Her sultry voice commanded. "Faster baby, faster."

Damn, woman, I'm going as fast as I can. He wanted to scream the words out but held back from telling her exactly what he thought of her. The babe he picked up at the bar was a one-night stand, a happily for now. That was it. Whether she got her rocks off or not was none of his concern. She wanted him, and after taking one look at her, he couldn't deny he wanted her too—at least for the night. His girlfriend didn't need to know.

Well,—she was technically his ex. Their on-again, off-again, whatever, was currently on hiatus. All thanks to a love note he spotted in her room, one sun-kissed morning after he took her in every position she desired. He could've sworn the howl that ripped from his throat, upon inspecting the unforgivable evidence of her treachery, had all of her neighbors calling nine-one-one. Yet, no emergency vehicles sounded. He made his getaway as soon as he found his clothes.

Now, Weldon was nestled inside a starlet who fell for his uncommonly handsome looks. He wasn't facetious or egotistical about his physical features. Not this time. Women, easily, fell for him, and he knew it. Finding a warm body was never an issue, and he never lacked for company.

"Right there, baby, oh yeah, oh yeah." She arched her back, popping up her large breasts to his delight. Her dusty rose tits danced across his eager irises. Yet, what she did next was *unexpected*.

Clawing at his back, she screamed—then she *faked it*.

"Oh baby, oh baby, oh baby. You're so strong. So good. *So* — fucking good."

Yes—he was. Yet this woman was putting on a big show. He watched her as she mouthed words that had nothing to do with her true feelings. The reason he sensed her complacence was a secret he'd never confess to her.

He grabbed ahold of her arms. Pinning them over her head, he rode her faster. His own marked pleasure, his ultimate goal. When the rehearsed panting hit his eardrums, he abruptly stopped. Lifting to his knees, he slipped out of her. Placing his hands on his hips, he stared with a wide smile.

"Why did you stop?"

Weldon shifted off the bed, his erection already softening. "You weren't enjoying yourself."

"Yes, I was."

He laughed. "If all the *oh baby's* were an indication, no, you were not."

She tugged at his arm. "Please, lover."

He snorted, then shook his head. "No. You can leave now."

She shouted. "What in the hell?"

"I know you're just trying to get back at your old flame, but you can't do that with me. Get out."

She scurried to a stand. His gaze shifted with the bouncing of her breasts. "You're right. I wanted to get back at the *m'effer,* but you don't need to dismiss me. Come back, and let's play."

He grabbed her clothing and tossed it at her nude form. "Good God, woman, didn't you hear me the first time? Here, take this and grab a cab home."

She looked down at the two twenty-dollar bills Weldon thrust at her. "Now you're paying me, like some whore?"

He lifted one eyebrow in response.

She huffed. "Well, I never." She snatched the bills from his hand and then quickly squirmed back into her clothes. He watched her, the corners of his mouth curling upward into a grin, his eyes glazed over with mischief as he caught her almost unintelligible mumbles of frustration. He held back the urge to chuckle, cracking his knuckles, instead, to take his mind off her sorry plight. As soon as he got rid of her, he'd take care of a few things, starting with a shower to wash her scent off him.

He threw his head back and roared with laughter when she slammed the door closed behind her. Widening his eyes, he then perked his ears up to listen out for any neighbors, awakened from the celebratory noise he made. His taut muscles relaxed as silence surrounded him. Glancing back at his phone on the nightstand, he considered calling Kara. She'd know what to do. The night of the full moon always gave him extra energy, and the event was only two days away. Yet, Weldon was feeling the effects already. Briefly, he considered what his brother was up to with his new girlfriend, Eva. After their unfavorable first few encounters, she and Weldon made up and were on speaking terms now. Still, he didn't consider her his future sister-in-law. Not yet—

Would Kara welcome him back? Maybe she'd allow a one-time fling, and then they'd go their separate ways again? Kara was always good in bed. He fingered the black, silk bed sheets and pictured her atop them, nude and smiling. Then he pictured the note from an admirer he'd found that morning. Kara had left Weldon shortly after giving him a mind-blowing bj.

He shook his head as he recalled her phone calls urging him to come back home so she could explain. Fuck that. Once a cheater, always a cheater. That was his motto. Besides, there were too many women in the world to explore. Why would he go back to one who proved unfaithful?

While Kingsley had searched for a mate, Weldon only wanted a female for the night. Still, the idea of a fated mate, for Weldon, fascinated him. Yet, who would tolerate his bullshit?

Weldon laughed with his own observation. He knew exactly who he was and how he came across to others. There weren't many who lingered in his presence, and even less he trusted. That was on purpose. The fewer memberships in his unwanted fan club, the better. The more friends one had, the more one had to lose. Remaining vigilant, on guard, observant and protective over everything in his life was something he already did due to what he was. He didn't need the extra drama of a tag-along girlfriend.

Still, a loyal, trustworthy, sexy female that wanted him just the way he was? That stayed by his side and cheered him on even when he was at his lowest? That craved him for more than the luxuries his money afforded. What would he do if he found her? He'd likely fall on his knees and beg her to stay, forever, for she'd prove to be a rare gem.

Sadly, he hadn't found her yet.

As good as Kara was between the sheets, even she knew she wasn't the one meant for him. Granted, he was young. Maybe there was still time.

Grabbing his shirt and pants, he slipped into his shoes, tossed his car keys into the air, and locked the door to his condo before he made his way down the long set of cement stairs. The night was young, and Weldon had extra time on his hands.

Locating his car in the building's garage, he pushed the start button and drove the canary yellow Corvette out, drawing in a deep breath as the wind whipped through his thick hair. He loved having the top down to the muscle car, relishing the beauty of the beast as he tested it on the highway at speeds nowhere within the posted limits. If there were any cops on the highway, he wanted them all female tonight. Women always fell for Weldon, no matter what their occupation.

Tonight, he had one goal. He drove to the far eastern portion of the state, heading toward the woods. There, he'd be able to work off some energy in the peace and quiet without any nosy neighbors or voyeurs ready to capture him on film. Current technology made it too easy to survey anyone. This made his nightly excursions dangerous. Weldon had to be careful. His life, and possibly his brothers' would be jeopardized if anyone knew his secret.

As he drove, his spirits lifted. Sniffing the unique scents surrounding him ranging from the asphalt below his tires, the scattered dewdrops on the leaves, and the musky scent from the nearby woods clouded his concentration and blessed his active mind with an addictive heady sensation. There was nothing more thrilling than rushing toward his natural habitat in a high-speed muscle car and throwing caution to the wind. If he never made it, he'd perish with a smile plastered across his face.

Winding his car to the natural curves of the road, he contemplated where else he might venture to at this late hour. A salacious smile quirked up the corners of his mouth as he pondered the possibilities. He knew exactly where he was headed. He only had to ride in the opposite direction from his original destination and then wait. His grin widened, the idea of catching his brother in the act whetting his appetite. As long as his brother didn't catch him—

Taking a hard right, he lowered the high beams and crept forward, sharpening his vision to keep track of his whereabouts in the dim lighting. With abundant green leaves and tall tree trunks at all angles, it was hard to tell exactly where he was without giving his location away. Not many cars ventured down the private path to the wooden cabin at the end of the road.

This was his older brother Kingsley's domain. It was his special place, and Weldon was invading it. Weldon chortled as he drove on.

Fifty minutes later, he parked the car off to one side of the house, gingerly opened his door, and then gently pressed it closed. He then snuck across the lawn to the living room window. Kingsley, an over-confident fellow, liked to leave the curtains open, figuring no one would walk up to his house and glance in. This time he was wrong. Weldon snuck a peek and widened his eyes, finding a naked Eva entwined with Kingsley beneath a thin sheet. He took one long, last look. Committing to memory, the heavy swell of her breasts and the smooth curve of her ass slipping out from underneath the thin fabric, wrapped mostly around her waist, before glancing away and snickering.

He tapped on the window, startling the two before rushing toward the front door, his heartbeat escalating with his rapid pace.

He stifled a cough, attempting to cover it up with the palm of his hand when the front door slammed open, hitting the brick wall next to him with a solid thud. Kingsley's mouth formed a long line of expletives, all directed at Weldon, while Weldon, casually, smiled.

"What in the hell are you doing here, and why didn't you call me first?"

Weldon smirked. "Brother, is that any way to treat your sibling?"

"Sibling, my ass! Right now,, you're an intruder, and I could shoot you if I owned a gun."

Weldon's gaze swept over Kingsley's body. "And some clothes. Do you always address your visitors buck naked?"

Weldon, suddenly, ducked as the light bulb overhead, cracked, and jagged edges of glass flew at him. He brushed the shards off his leather jacket and glanced up to find Eva standing behind Kingsley.

Weldon shouted at her over Kingsley's shoulder. "Did you do that? What a way to welcome your guests."

She swept a strand of Kingsley's hair over his left ear. "I could say the same for you. We were having a private moment." Kingsley grabbed Eva around the waist and pulled her to him with a wide grin.

Weldon's gaze swept over the long, fluffy robe Eva wore. "Close your curtains, then."

Kingsley grumbled. "Is there something you wanted, Weldon?"

Weldon waved his hand in the air. "Nah. I was just seeing what my brother was up to. Now I've seen enough." Weldon swiveled on his heel and walked away.

Kingsley retorted. "Smartass."

Weldon strode, uninterrupted, toward his car. "Takes one to know one."

"Don't come back unless you're in danger or on fire."

Weldon guffawed, giving Kingsley a backward wave as he turned the corner. "You'll never see me then."

Catching Eva and Kingsley in a compromising position was the best thing he did all day. He slumped into his car, ready for the next adventure. His thoughts returned to Kara. Where was she now? After his misfortune with the girl back at the bar-the one who faked every expression while they were in bed-could he call Kara for the quickie he never received? The one he deserved after the day from hell.

He texted her before he shifted the car in reverse. Then he peeled out of Kingsley's terrain onto the main road.

Whatcha doing? Want to get together?

That was simple enough and to the point. If Kara didn't get his meaning, that was her fault. He would just have to do without sex tonight.

Almost at his destination, his phone rattled a familiar tune he hadn't heard in a long while. He forgot he gave Kara her own jingle. Holding the phone up to his face, he unlocked it with the latest facial recognition software. He then blinked several times, attempting to clear his view to discover her reply.

Where are you?

He pulled the phone up to his lips and talked into it as words popped up across his screen. Then, he pressed the arrow at the end of the sentence to send his reply in the form of a text message.

Meet me in the woods if you want some.

Weldon made no pretenses. He usually got what he wanted. If one female was unwilling to deliver, another one would do, just as well. Being a member of his kind, he never lacked female companionship. The necessity to hunt one down or search for one was a foreign concept to him. He never understood the plight of human males, worrying and concerned they'd never find the elusive *one*. Why search for that singular female when there were so many available? Any able body would do.

Drawn to his savage, inner being, women found themselves, quickly rendered defenseless, unable to do much else but lie down and succumb to whatever he desired. He entertained the idea that they were, only, submitting to his natural, sensual charm. He knew his inner beast and possibly musky pheromones played a bigger part in their refusal to fight. He never met a woman that resisted him though the idea of finding one greatly appealed to him.

For now, Weldon was satisfied with his one-nightstands and haphazard excursions. Speaking of which—he calculated the distance remaining to the woods. His current location meant Kara would make it to the forest faster than he would. He stepped on the gas pedal, forcing his car to top speed before issuing a command into his phone, watching the words as they formed across the screen in a text message to Kara.

Take your clothes off when you get there and hide. I will find you.

The thrill of chasing her raw scent through damp, thick forest and tall, foreboding trees until he discovered her, pounced on her, and had his way with her, revved up his heartbeat to full throttle. There was nothing more enticing to his kind than hunting down prey.

Kara had a target on her—only, she didn't know it yet.

Chapter Two

What in the hell was she doing in the forest? And with Weldon? They had their chance.

She blew it, and he walked away. Yet here he was texting her for a booty call. She should've said no—yet Kara couldn't let go of the chance to be surrounded, again, by Weldon's manly, muscular body, if only for a brief moment. Weldon was, easily, the best lover she ever had. She missed him. She had chastised herself several times after he slammed the door on their future.

Only an innocent exploration, it snowballed, quickly, into something else.

His name was Jack. He was a co-worker. They constantly flirted on the job. But she never thought it would go any further until he wrote her a note, opening his heart to her and telling her of his real interest in dating her. The fact that she had a boyfriend should've deterred Jack, but it didn't. Yet, Weldon found the note. It was the first time she begged anyone to stay.

On her hands and knees with tears streaming down her face, she gave Weldon one last gift before he went away- the longest, biggest bj of his life. Slowing down then speeding up, she imagined he'd stay. Forgiving her flirtation that led to the impromptu love note, she found tossed among her things in her leather messenger bag. After she worked him for long, arduous minutes that had her gagging and gasping for air, she

12

watched him and then waited for a response. Yet, he simply sat on the edge of the bed, amidst the silence, gathering his breath and his strength. He then thanked her and, promptly, walked out of her life. Stunned, she watched him disappear while her heart dropped like an anvil straight to her stomach.

So, why was she standing in the forest, peeling her clothes off her body, ready to find a hiding place? She shook her head at her current situation. She should be at home, instead. Yet, letting Weldon walk out of her life was the biggest mistake she ever made- that, and encouraging Jake's interest.

Jake was handsome. Nothing made that fact any less real. Yet, Weldon was—incredible, unlike any man she dated before. With his sexy, brash, overconfident personality, his bad-ass car, and his killer physique, there wasn't much about him Kara disliked. The only problem proved to be that Weldon's decisions were usually final.

Weldon decided they were through. Kara aimed to do whatever she needed to change his mind.

A half-hour later, her heart almost stopped when she spotted his car pulling underneath a nearby tree. *Damn.* Lost in her thoughts, she forgot his last request. She needed to run.—and now.

Accustomed only to the occasional jog, she sprinted with all her might. Her heart rapidly beat, accelerating to unearthly levels. The precious organ pumped blood to her extremities and threatened to burst forth from her body. Instead of taking care not to slip or squeak across the dewy leaves and grass, she ignored the desperate plight, alerting him of her presence. Her casual, sparkly sneakers, a mistake she instantly regretted at this moment, were designed more for a glamorous runway than a marathon in the woods.

The tedious task of remaining upright was a tough one. As she continued her desperate need to place distance between her and her lover, her legs no longer seemed attached to her body. Both limbs, having a mind of their own, broke free from her several strained seconds ago in an attempt to escape the man she wanted desperately to immerse in. Next time she'd have to re-think her footwear.

Free of her confining bra, her breasts bounced and swayed as she zipped past small patches of tall trees and around confounding prickly bushes. She heard a voice in the distance. Was Weldon counting? She stopped, heaving in lung fulls of air and attempting to discern what the man said. He was! Impossibly, Weldon was counting down. She heard his knuckles crack and a rush of sound before she took off once again.

Searching around her, she sought out quick places to hide but found none. Out in the middle of nowhere, she was as exposed to him as a deer to a hunter's rifle. As she moved, her thigh, suddenly, brushed against a thick, protruding stick, slicing a small slit across her soft skin, near the knee. She smashed her hand against the tear when she found a large, full bush and decided the game was over. She'd hide behind it and hope for the best.

Praying she wouldn't step barefoot into a nest of fire ants or worse, she bent low, making sure her nude form was fully covered by the foliage. Taking big swallows, she worked on her breath. Trying to slow the intake. Dredging up an image in her mind of her accelerated heartbeats returning to normal. She'd never played this game with Weldon before. Maybe he was no good at it.

She waited. Inhaling a deep breath, her body relaxed. She welcomed coveted tranquility flowing through her taut nerves. Her senses, once heightened and on edge, eased. She closed her eyes briefly and breathed out a sigh of relief until she heard a low growl. Her eyelids flipped open, her eyes widening as she attempted to discern what in the hell was in the darkness surrounding her. Was it close? Was it feral? Oh, God! Where in the hell was Weldon?

Something pushed her forward and pinned her to the ground. She uttered a silent scream. It whispered words into her ear.

"Caught you."

When his hot breath caressed across her earlobe, she knew, immediately, who was on top of her. Weldon flipped her to face him. She caught his widening grin.

"You're naked. Good. No time wasted on pleasantries, then. I like it."

She caressed the red-colored paisley bandana he wore under his bike helmet. It was simple headwear- an item found in any dollar store. Weldon wore it as an act of rebellion. It symbolized the freedom of the open road and the vastness of nature awaiting his exploration.

"I see you've been riding," she said softly. His sensual lips curved up in response. Unlike her preference for air conditioning and cushioned chairs, Weldon loved the outdoors. The more rugged the establishment, the happier he was.

He sat up, the majority of his weight resting on his knees. She watched him strip off his clothing, gasping aloud when his manhood sprung alive from his tight jeans. With one quick swoop, he pulled her up, resting her thighs across his own, and then plunged into her. Tossing her head back, she rolled her eyes with his all too familiar mixed scent of sweat and manly musk. He bounced her atop him as she squealed, welcoming every one of his powerful thrusts as he took them to a pleasurable, inevitable conclusion.

Her mouth flapped open. Her useless lips tried to form his name. Instead, it issued heavy pants and long moans of approval.

He brushed his cheek against hers. "Kara. Dear, sweet Kara, we were always good at this."

He was right. She never had any complaints regarding his love-making skills. Yet, this wasn't love-making. This was downright hedonistic sex. She wanted more.

She shot up a heavenward spiral of ecstasy as he plunged into her one last time and then stilled, holding her tight within his arms while his body shuddered. She forced a lazy smile upon her face as he released, happy that in his haste to get to her, he hadn't rolled on his usual latex protection. He pivoted off her with a sigh.

Kara scooted toward him, snuggling underneath one strong arm. "Mmmm. That was good. I could go for another."

He glanced over at her and chuckled. "Maybe in a little bit."

She caressed the tip of her finger down his cheek. "I miss you."

He swiveled up onto his elbow. His eyebrows furrowed together. "Look, this was just us scratching an itch. Don't make it out to be more than it is."

She looked into his eyes. "Don't you miss me?"

"Darling, you cheated on me."

"No, I didn't."

He sat up, shoving one arm in front of him in a gesture to stop. "Look, it's over and done with. There's no going back."

"But I didn't cheat on you, Weldon."

"What about Jack?"

"He just interpreted my friendliness wrong. I never had an interest in him." Well, maybe she did have an interest in Jack, but she wasn't going to tell Weldon that.

"Kara, our time is over."

"Please, Weldon. Don't discard me because of some nonsense. I did nothing wrong."

He stared at her for a long time before he stood up. Wiping the soil and grass off his corded thighs and firm butt, she watched his manhood dangle between his legs, silently willing it to stand at attention once more so she could pounce on him and give him an encore presentation.

"Kara—I don't know."

"Give me a chance, Weldon. I won't let you down."

He grimaced. "We'll have to see what happens. I can't guarantee anything."

Her eyes widened. "Seriously? You'll give me a chance?"

He shook one hand in the air in front of her. "Dating, Kara. I can't promise anything else."

She ran toward him. Throwing her arms around his neck, she planted a sloppy, open-mouthed kiss onto his lips. Her hands swirled lazy circles down his chest while a saucy smile plastered across her face. "One more for the road?"

The corners of his mouth slid up into a grin. "Why not?"

She dropped to her knees and found Weldon's eyebrows lifted in curiosity. The golden flecks sparkling from his mischievous irises, somehow, seemed brighter.

Her fingers surrounded him. "Here, let me help you." She dropped her gaze and focused her concentration. He threw his head back and groaned.

KARA LIFTED ONTO WELDON'S chest and sighed. At some point during their amorous tryst, the red bandana on his head lowered. It was now knotted around his neck like a handkerchief.

"I have to head home, or my roommate will worry and wonder where I'm at. I ran out of the place so fast, I don't think I left a note. I might've received a message by now."

Weldon quirked up an eyebrow. "Roommate?"

"Yeah, I have a roommate. A lot has happened since we broke up, you know."

"Male or female?"

"Female."

He nodded. So that's where the unfamiliar scent came from. It was faint but sweet and, if he was honest, a bit enticing. Definitely a scent he never encountered before. He knew it wasn't Kara's, but he wondered where she picked it up. He figured she must've brushed up against some sort of fruit or other delicacies in a supermarket or store. The idea that her roommate produced such an alluring perfume had him baffled, speechless, and wanting to rush back to Kara's apartment to get to know her. Would Kara take him home tonight to meet this infamous flower?

Kara slipped her panty, shorts, and shoes on. She grabbed her shirt while Weldon stared at her, his mouth gaping open in surprise when Kara didn't look at him. "I gotta go," she shouted over her shoulder while her feet moved toward the car.

"Wait."

Kara swiveled toward him when she reached the driver's side door. She fumbled with her bra, attempting to connect the small metal hooks with a slight grimace. She then shrugged the t-shirt over her, pulling it down over her belly when Weldon approached. She tilted her head and looked up at him. "What is it? I gotta go." She thumbed at her car.

He shook his head. "Never mind. I'll call you."

She swung the door open. "Yeah, you do that." Slipping into the driver's seat, she peered over at him before she slammed the door and turned on the ignition. "It was good, Weldon, really good. I'm so glad we're back together. I'll talk to you soon, babe."

Weldon scrubbed a hand through his thick hair as she drove onto the dirt road, away from him. "Oh hell. Now she thinks we're an item." It's what he feared when he offered the option. Dating, for Kara, likely meant any interest he might've had in another female was out.

He lifted to a stand. Stretching his arms out to either side of him, he splayed open his fingers. He arched his spine, enjoying the cool temperature sweeping lazy swirls across his nude body. He threw his head back and uttered a low growl as the change overtook him. Falling to all fours, he relished in the rush of switching to his true form. Fur sprouted where there was none before. His face elongated into a full snout, and his teeth lengthened. He unhinged his jaw and expanded it to capacity, his nostrils flaring and drawing in the various scents he picked up in the depth of forest surrounding him. Everything seemed clearer and brighter in his primary beast's form.

One single fang slipped out beneath his upper lip, betraying his impurity. Only one person knew his true identity, and it wasn't his brother, Kingsley.

He leaped forward, his legs breaking into a run, his heartbeat accelerating with the rapid pace and the thrill of freedom. Yet was he truly free? Would Kara let him explore other options? Or would she tie herself to him, squeezing out of him all the oxygen available, making sure he'd never leave her side again? He growled loudly. His body slammed the ground. His lungs worked overtime, wheezing out bits of air while his heart did double duty, pumping blood through its chambers. Damn. What in the hell did he get himself into?

He screeched to a stop beside an unusually tall tree, dropped his head back, and uttered a long, mournful howl.

A FEW WEEKS LATER, Kara invited him over to her apartment, an opportunity he figured he'd never get. After living an unexpected monogamous life for two harrowing weeks, he was ready to break free. Still, Weldon didn't want to end things with Kara the way he always ended relationships. He wanted to remain friends. Yet, each time he brought up the subject, she shut it down with a cheery smile and an overly positive comment regarding how happy she was to be back with Weldon. Reminding her that he only offered to date her did nothing to budge her steely reserve. She wasn't giving up, and she was never letting him go. Weldon never expected to end up a prisoner.

He liked Kara, and he loathed the idea of hurting her as she, once, hurt him. Still, too much time had passed since they were last together, and he no longer felt the way he did before. Trudging to her doorway, he resolved to break it off with her despite the heavy sadness surrounding his heart. Intense images floated across his mind at her expected reaction to his news. He put one foot in front of the other over the impossibly long, carpeted hallway. Left-right-left-right. He plodded forward and then, abruptly, stopped as a rush of something extraordinary filled his nostrils.

Everything in him suddenly vibrated and tingled. He clenched his fingers and balled them into fists as he took one deep whiff of something incredible. He whined low upon exhale, uncaring who heard the inhuman sound. Then he laughed. A seemingly maniacal yet giddy sound springing forth from his lips as the sweet sensational smell swirled through his heart and uplifted the corners of his mouth into a full grin.

Holy hell. What in blazes was that delicious scent? And where was it coming from?

The sensual perfume wafted across his taught nerves. It teased every fiber of his being and strummed across the final chords of his willpower as it tempted him to knock upon every single door in the hallway. If only to find out who owned the magnificent scent that threatened to bring him to his knees.

Damn it, Weldon. Get it together. He chastised himself until he, unwittingly, inhaled another breath of air and groaned. His head dropped to his chest, and he issued short whines for mercy. His legs silently urged him to turn back. To run in the opposite direction despite his innate need to claim and possess whoever belonged to the magic potion that would make his life complete.

Was this what the elders meant? Was this the fabled curse that was brought upon his kind? His brother definitely, wouldn't use the word *curse* to describe what he discovered with Eva. Yet, Weldon had never found his fated one. He considered the possibility and, mostly, laughed at the idea but seriously contemplated it? No.

Yet, lingering in the middle of the hallway, he found it harder and harder to stand the more he inhaled the magical potion meant for him. He stumbled to a nearby wall and then slid to the floor. He attempted to relax his wild, rapid heartbeats with his breaths, now mere attempts to wheeze in life-sustaining oxygen. Yet every time he inhaled slowly, a long low whine accompanied each exhale.

Damn. What in the hell was he going to do? He was only here to pick up Kara for their date. He found himself, weakened and on the ground, pining for a stranger in one of the apartments on her floor. He gazed at the multitude of colors in the paisley carpet, trying to determine his next move. The seat of his pants betrayed him, tenting with the magnificent, unique scent swirling through his insides. The irresistible perfume rushed through him, crumbling every barrier he had created. Strengthening the lost hope, he didn't know still lingered within him for his very own mate. The wispy, perfect tendrils invaded every inch of his inner being, leaving blissful happiness in its wake. If he found *her*, she'd have to run. He was ready to claim her, although Kara waited for him in her apartment.

Weldon forced himself up and lifted to a stand. His inner beast clawed its way to the forefront as the intense urge to claim and dominate stirred his libido and tightened his muscles. His next move might prove to be his last. Regardless . he had to find out where the delicious scent originated. Trudging to the end of the hallway, he sniffed by each door, aware that, at any moment, someone could pop open one of the doors and surprise both the resident and him. If caught, the stranger would likely yell at him or punch him in the face. Both options seemed a fair trade for his ability to solve the mysterious origin of the delicious scent.

Until he found the scent's source, the rest of the night was on hold. Kara might be upset that he was running late, but there was no way he would let this opportunity pass him by. Not when he had the chance to find *her*.

Eight strong whiffs later, and he ended up back at Kara's doorway. It was impossible. Yet, the tantalizing, knee-weakening potion stemmed from her. *No, not from her.* Unless she bought an amazing perfume recently, or she was cooking a stellar meal, Weldon knew for a fact what he sought wasn't from her. He lifted his hand to knock on the door, a puzzled expression coloring his demeanor when it swung open, and the most gorgeous female he'd ever spotted suddenly appeared.

Heavenly angels! Who was this?

A beautiful sound sprung from the jezebel's saucy, parted lips. "Can I help you?"

He swallowed back the urge to shout *yes*, tamping down other parts of him that sprang to life at her mere presence.

Good Gods, where did this woman come from?

"I'm Weldon." Sticking a handout to shake didn't seem good enough. He wanted to pull her into him, fondle her entire body, and whisper into her soft, delicate ear, "Where have you been all my life?" He'd follow up his question with sweet promises that would soon turn erotic.

His breaths trembled upon receiving her melodic reply. "Oh, you're dating my roommate."

The realization of what she said was like a smack to his forehead. *She was the roommate? Oh lord. He was in trouble.*

Suddenly lightheaded, he staggered backward, instantly aware of what he must look like in the presence of the dark-haired Goddess.

She took a step forward to possibly assist him and then stopped as if she realized that Weldon was ultimately a stranger. "Are you okay?"

He attempted to nod, but the gesture threw him more off balance. Drawing in a lungful of air, he immediately regretted it when her luscious scent swirled through him. His knees buckled beneath him. Instinctively, he grabbed for the wall. He grunted as his useless fingers slipped down the worn paint with his utter failure. His back slammed into the carpet.

She squealed and immediately rushed to his side, bending her angelic face over his. "Are you okay? Shit. Can you stand up?" She offered him her soft, gentle arm but all he could do was stare at her perfect, striking features, committing to memory the delicate angle of her jaw, the perfect, full lushness of her beautiful lips, and the stunning golden-brown eyes filled with kindness staring back at him, waiting for him to answer her.

His body overheated while his fingers stretched toward her, desperate to grab ahold of the girl with the sultry scent splayed across him. Yet, he did the opposite of what his beast cried out for him to do. Gritting his teeth, he slid his tongue over the back of the one fang that threatened to slip out from its confined area, exposing more than he was willing to reveal. Then he closed his eyes and silently willed her to disappear before he did something he'd regret.

Chapter Three

"**K**ara!" Tania shouted, hoping her roommate would stop doing whatever she was doing at the moment to tend to her boyfriend. The term boyfriend seemed a weak description for the chiseled, delicious beefcake lying on the floor in front of her. She knew Kara had a man in her life, but she never knew he looked like this.

He was quite remarkable. She tried to look away, but her eyes seemed glued to the roped muscles of his impossibly lean stomach peeking out from beneath his solid, red-colored shirt. When Tania touched him, wanting to discover if he was okay, she felt the dip and sway of his washboard abs as he sucked in an inhale. Her hand, instinctively, shot back toward her before she had the chance to fully enjoy the follow-through of his exhale.

Damn, the guy was sexy as hell.

Her gaze swept over his fine, chiseled features adorning his aristocratic features. How had she never bumped into him before? Moose Creek was a fairly small town, and there were only so many bars. —Still, maybe he didn't drink? *Nah.* With a body like that, it was more likely he frequented them. Besides, Kara loved hanging out at bars. And he belonged to Kara. Still, Tania had met her share of single men in the town, but she'd never met him. He didn't seem like the type of man a woman was likely to forget.

Kara rushed to his side before she had the chance to contemplate further where the delicious man came from. Tania breathed in a sigh of relief as she switched places with Kara, happy to return to the living room. By now, Weldon had opened his eyes and was speaking to her roommate. He was okay. Tania planned to continue what she was doing before. What was that again?

Kara pulled him into the room, tossing him onto the couch and taking a seat beside him. Tania stared at him, taking the opportunity to rake her gaze over him, unnoticed.

My oh my. What a delicious man. Too bad he was taken. Not that she'd do anything to change the situation if he was available. Tania didn't delve into relationships. All men cheated, lied, and made false promises. It wasn't worth keeping one stringing along when they'd only end up disappointing her. Whenever she needed male companionship, or better yet, a much-needed fling, men were always around, especially at her place of work. Granted, her job didn't always draw the best of the rest, but when she was horny, she wasn't all that choosy.

Yet the guy on her couch named Weldon? Wow. What a stunner! She pondered why Kara didn't tell her how flawlessly beautiful he was on the outside. Tania knew the man had blemishes on the inside. She had listened to enough of Kara's stories to pinpoint exactly what his faulty parts were, most of them resulting from his cocky, assertive attitude. Sadly, a man who knew the effect he had on women was never a good thing.

Kara brushed past her and into the kitchen. She ran a washcloth underwater and then promptly returned to Weldon's side, placing it across his forehead. He swept it aside.

"I'm not dying, just wounded," Weldon said. He then inhaled, rolled his eyes back into his head, and then collapsed into the sofa with a low groan. Well. —maybe he didn't roll his eyes that far back, but it sure looked like it to Tania. The poor guy, apparently, wasn't feeling well.

Kara leaned over him, concern knitting her eyebrows together. "Are you sure you're okay?"

Weldon didn't respond. During the ensuing silence, Tania's cellphone chimed. She started for the phone, reaching out to grab it with one hand when her big toe skidded across the kitchen tile, almost tripping her in the process. Out of the corner of her eye, she caught Weldon's sudden movement. His body jerked awkwardly, like a marionette coming to life while his eyelids popped open. His head swiveled in her direction, his attention strangely focused on her. Seconds later, he slowly sunk back into the sofa pillows when she checked her footing and picked up the call.

"Hello?" The ensuing phone conversation had Tania scampering to her bedroom and closing the door behind her. She ended the call a minute or two later, shrugging her curvy body into dark-colored pants and a V-neck top. Male patrons enjoyed the brief peep show they received during their scant moments spent with her. She noticed her tips increased with the plunge of her blouses. Granted, this didn't always make her comfortable. Tania veered more on the conservative side than the skanky.

Spritzing her favorite perfume over her wrists and between her breasts, she took one last appreciative glance at herself in the mirror before cautiously entering the living room. If the lovebirds were sprawled across the sofa, naked, she'd make a break for the front door without a second glance. Well, maybe just one stare to fully gawk at what she knew she'd find: Weldon's well-developed, mouth-watering buttocks. That's if he wasn't hiding the firm, round globes from her avid curiosity.

What she found instead surprised her. Weldon sat back on the sofa, his arms spread across the back of it. His gaze shot toward her as she walked through her doorway. It scoured her form, slowly and thoroughly, from the top of her head to the tips of her toes. He then returned to look at her face. A sound like a low growl emitted from his throat, and she could've sworn a tooth, possibly an incisor, slipped out from beneath his right upper lip.

"So, you're Tania. Kara's roommate."

Tania could've sworn she introduced herself to him, but then again, he had taken a hard hit to the ground. Maybe he didn't remember the introduction. She stopped in mid-track and nodded in reply. Conscious of the minutes ticking by, her feet urged her to make her escape, but she didn't want to seem rude.

"How long have you lived here?"

From anyone else, it would've been a normal question, but the way Weldon bit the words out as if accusing her of some wrongdoing made Tania not want to answer him.

"Two weeks. Why?"

She caught Weldon's look of surprise. "You moved in two weeks ago?"

She clutched her purse to her chest and took a step toward the front door. "Yes, why? Have I done something wrong? Why this interrogation?"

A smile quirked up the corners of Weldon's mouth, curving it upward into impossible lengths.

He chuckled. "You're fiery, aren't you?"

What in the hell? Was he mocking her? She gritted her teeth and glared at him.

"What is your problem?"

He laughed at her. "Listen, princess, I ask because your scent is so engrained in this apartment. You couldn't have been here a mere two weeks. If so, you must've done a helluva lot of other stuff for it to get into all of the furniture. Know what I mean?" He waggled his eyebrows.

"Why, you cocky bastard! First of all, I don't have to answer any of your questions. Where is Kara anyway? Someone needs to be babysitting you!"

"She's taking a shower."

"Well then, maybe you should join her. Oh, and by the way, my sex life, frequency, and where I have sex is my damn business, not yours. If I want to have sex all over this place, as long as Kara doesn't care, you have no opinion."

She slammed the door, muttering under her breath as she walked away. "Damn prick." She could've sworn she heard his boisterous laughter as she picked up her steps, thankful to escape his grueling presence.

WELDON FIDDLED WITH a meatball on his plate, twirling the spaghetti intermittently on his fork as he spoke. "So, who is this, Tania?"

Kara lifted her fork to her lips and scrunched her eyebrows together before taking a bite of the food. "What do you mean?"

"I mean, where do you know her from? How did she become your roommate? Did you advertise for one, or did you meet her and then decide to have her move in?"

Kara giggled. "Why? Do you want to replace her?"

Weldon dropped his fork and stared at her. He remained speechless, unable to reply to her inquiry. All he wanted from Kara were answers.

She enjoyed another forkful of ravioli. "I'm just kidding."

It didn't matter if Kara was teasing him or not. He had no interest in moving forward with their relationship, especially when he realized his mate occupied the room next to Kara's.

"Tell me about Tania."

Kara dropped her fork onto her plate and reached for her glass. "Do you think she's a criminal or something?" She gulped back a long swig before slamming her glass back onto the table.

"Why won't you answer my questions?"

"Why are you so interested?"

He shrugged his shoulders and lied. "I'm not. I just want to know more about the woman who's sharing an apartment with the woman I'm dating."

She smiled. "Oh, that makes sense. Getting protective of me? I like it." She returned her napkin to her lap. "I met her through a friend. She seemed nice and needed a new place to live—trouble with an old boyfriend—or so she said. I took her in. I needed the money anyway, and she seems like a good person."

"How do you know she's going to pay the rent and that she's not using you to get away from her ex?"

Kara snorted. "Well, no one really knows that. She works, though. She's a bartender at Shenanigans. I think she makes good money, too."

Weldon looked down at his plate. His memory kicked into high speed as he flipped through recollections of women he'd taken to bed, including the numerous bartenders he'd enjoyed. He willed the rising panic within him to stop. He coaxed the tense nerves and taught muscles to relax, easing them with the sudden realization that if he had slept with her, there was no way in hell he'd forget her.

She was a gem. A jewel to treasure. It wasn't only her scent that excited him. The fact that she loathed him already had his balls tightening and the front of his pant tenting at awkward moments throughout the night. Weldon loved a challenge. Tania presented that to him in Kara's apartment when she scolded him and then walked out the door. Images of how he'd like to punish the wanton female flipped through his mind and drew a smile across his lips. One day he'd engage in his fantasies with the bewitching vixen, but first, he wanted to know more about her.

"Maybe I should question her. Make sure she's a good person."

Kara stopped jabbing bits of ravioli on her plate and looked at him. "What? Why?"

"She's only been with you two weeks."

"Weldon, she's not a serial killer. She's fine. But if you must interrogate her, you can do so at her job."

"Shenanigans, right?"

Kara nodded.

"When does she work again?"

"She was called in tonight, but she'll be there tomorrow night, too, from seven p.m. to midnight." Kara chewed on a morsel of food, swallowed it down, and then tilted her head to one side. "You're really going to talk to her?"

"I think I should."

"As my boyfriend?"

"I'm not your boyfriend, Kara."

Kara waved her fork between them. "Well, this is boyfriend stuff you're doing."

If Kara only knew Weldon wasn't interested in her, not after meeting her roommate. And after his inquiry at Shenanigans, he'd have to find a way to break it off with Kara without inciting her rage.

Thankfully, Kara didn't understand the intent of Weldon's questions and his fascination with her roommate. If she did, the night and their supper would've been ruined. She blew off his questions as silly fun instead of what they were meant to be: a tactical maneuver to subtly find out more. Kara openly talked about Tania, telling Weldon what she knew about her during the next ten minutes. After Kara's candid disclosure, Weldon discovered Tania was much like him—she dated but didn't settle down. This unnerved him. The last thing he wanted was to snatch her between bedmates. Kara said something about Tania having her heartbroken years ago by a guy who was unfaithful. *Cad.* Who, in their right mind, would leave Tania for another? The louse must've lost his marbles. He definitely, lost Tania. This made Weldon smile. She didn't need to be with someone unworthy of her.

Weldon's eyebrows shot up when Kara confided that Tania spent barely two days in their apartment in the last two weeks. Kara confessed it as a good thing, favoring her privacy over having an apartment buddy, but Weldon couldn't help silently questioning where Tania spent her nights.

Kara waggled her eyebrows. "Are you ready for dessert?"

Weldon grimaced with the thought of Kara lying across her silk bed sheets with a come-hither look in her eyes. Her red high heels with little else on, she invited Weldon to join her with a generous sweep of her hands.

Weldon shook his head at the vivid image. After meeting Tania, he had no other option. He had to refuse Kara's invitation. Besides, he wouldn't be able to get his body to work when all he wanted now was Tania between the sheets, preferably in *his* bed. Weldon emitted a low growl and then stopped when he spotted Kara's raised eyebrows.

"Well—I guess dessert is on."

"No."

The word struck Kara hard. His beast sensed it with the sudden stutter to her heartbeats. She stared at him, a shocked expression gracing her pretty face while her blood ran cold.

"What? You don't want me?"

He lowered his voice. "Kara, I told you we were only dating. I'm not sure this is going to work out. We used to be together, and it didn't work out then. There's no difference between then and now."

"Why did you lead me on?"

"I didn't. I told you exactly what we were. I never promised anything else. You've built a fantasy about us in your mind. You know somewhere deep inside you that we won't work out. Admit it, Kara. I'm not the same man. I can't commit to you any longer. I would just end up breaking your heart."

Kara hanged her head and sighed. After several long seconds, she nodded. "You're right. I really wanted it to work this time, but you're correct. You're different, and so am I. We'd never work."

"Let's just walk away as friends."

"Okay." Kara's admittance stunned Weldon for a few long seconds. He expected her anger, as before. He was pleased she understood.

Kara lifted from her seat. She allowed Weldon's hug.

He whispered into her hair. "I want you to find that right one, for you. It's not me."

"Yes."

He swiped at a few tears streaming from her eyes. After walking her to her car, he strolled to his Vette, secluded two blocks away from the restaurant, hiding from inquisitive eyes. At least, that was his intent. The color yellow stood out among the common, almost bland colors of cars produced. That's why he chose it. Yet, the striking yellow would never be mistaken or used for camouflage.

Almost to his car, his sensitive ears picked up on an unusual sound, one that shouldn't be heard on a near-empty street. He turned in time to find two men rushing him in the darkness, their shoes squeaking against the sidewalk. The look on their faces clearly defined their intent. They were not here to make friends.

Weldon hunched his shoulders and gritted his teeth. An image of the fictional character, Wolverine, entering his head for a split second before his nails extended to claws. He slashed at the male directly in front of him before the man had the chance to bring the metal pipe in his hands down. The useless object clanged against the concrete, forgotten as the man grabbed at his throat, a look of distress coloring across his reddened face.

The man's accomplice stopped and gasped while he gazed at his buddy, struggling to catch his next breath of air as blood gushed like cascading streams between his trembling fingers. The intact male turned toward Weldon and shouted. "What in the hell are you?"

Weldon curled his index finger and beckoned him with a rolling growl. "Come here and find out."

"Hell no." The man swiveled on his heel and ran in the opposite direction. Weldon ignored him, for now, and focused on the man in front of him falling to his knees. Weldon grinned, his canine teeth lengthening and sharpening, preparing for the next step. He pounced on the male, holding him still as his body tried to crumple to the floor.

"So, you thought you could steal from me, huh? Well, aren't you surprised that I'm the one taking everything from you?" Weldon shoved the man's hands out of the way, exposing the gorgeous artery overflowing with the man's essence. He drew in a long whiff of the sensual perfume scenting the air. He then threw his head back and opened his jaw, the white of his teeth glinting amidst the darkness. With a quick downward turn, he descended upon the man. He gouged his neck, his fangs sinking further and deeper through the flesh, slicing through the tender nerves and muscles below like boiled pasta. He inhaled and exhaled rapidly as he siphoned the man's blood, his heartbeat jolting alive with sudden renewed energy. He relished in the contrasting cool breeze ruffling through his damp hair and the warm liquid rushing down his eager throat. Every time he took a human, it was an indescribable thrill.

He didn't often satisfy his secondary beast with what it craved most. When he did, the beast thanked him with near orgasmic sensations which passed through him like thick waves over a famished, scorched beach. He grunted as the man withered beneath him, his body almost spent of the liquid gold Weldon's secondary beast needed. The man's eyes rolled to the back of his head. His body, quickly turning cold, twitched, and writhed within his grasp. Weldon opened his fingers and let the guy's lifeless form slide over the concrete when he was done. He wiped the excess liquid from the corners of his mouth, sliding a knuckle between his lips to enjoy the remainder of the man's gift. Realizing his meal was done more quickly than expected, he whined as he pulled his hand away until he remembered there was one more. The one who questioned what Weldon was.

He stood up, brushed the dirt off his pants, and closed his eyes. Scanning his immediate area, he engaged his hearing and heightened sense of smell to locate nemesis number two. His lips broke into a wide grin when he found him.

Standing to his full height, he arched his back and stretched his hands above him with a blissful sigh. Twisting his neck side to side, he reveled in the satisfying cracking sound before he prepared for round two. Time to catch another criminal. He'd devour him like he did his partner. Falling to all fours, he let his primary beast take over. He threw his head back, howled, and then ran toward his second course.

Chapter Four

"**A**nd what will you have?"

Weldon looked up at the lovely bartender asking him the question. If the circumstances were different, he knew exactly what he'd order.

Tania's jaw dropped. "What happened to you?" She leaned over the counter to get a better look at the left side of his face. "My, that's a shiner. I haven't seen one of those in years." She tipped back to stand on her heels. "Need some ice? I can get you an ice pack. Come with me."

Weldon waved off her suggestion. "No, I'm good. I'm a fast healer."

"Did you get into a fight? Did Kara deck you?" Tania laughed. "Good for her."

Weldon grimly replied. "We're not together anymore."

"What? You were this morning." Tania pointed her finger at him. "Did you do anything to hurt her? I mean, I don't know you, but I can just see you doing something."

Weldon threw his hands up in the air. "The bruise is not from Kara. And our break-up was a mutual decision. Okay? It happened tonight, at dinner."

Tania didn't reply. Instead, she looked at him for several long seconds as if she were trying to figure him out. Her eyes narrowed, and she had a stark look of judgment plastered across her face. Finally, she grabbed a bar towel, rubbed the area in front of her with it, and then spoke. "Okay. I can imagine Kara's in pain. I'll have to change my plans for tonight and go home."

"Oh? Were you heading somewhere after work?"

Tania's head shot up. "It's none of your damn business."

Weldon threw his hands up in the air in a show of surrender. "Okay. I get it. Listen, I think we got off on the wrong foot. Can we start again?"

"Why?"

"Because I like you."

She wrinkled her nose. "You don't know me."

"Yes, but I like your spunk and your personality. And —you're pretty."

She stared at him. "You're kidding, right?" She turned her head to acknowledge a patron, indicating she'd be right there. "Look, I have to get back to work. Are you ordering or not?"

"I'll have a cold beer."

"What brand?"

Weldon grinned. "Surprise me."

She chuckled. "You are something —"

He held his hand out to her. "Hi. I'm Weldon. I'm an asshole but an all-around good guy, most of the time. And you are?"

The corners of her mouth quirked up into a smile. She placed her hand within his larger one and returned his handshake.

"Probably doing the wrong thing. I'm Tania, the bartender. I'll go get you that beer."

Weldon watched her depart, his gaze traveling further down her back until it hit her curvy ass. *My, what a sweet temptation.* To feel, caress and squeeze her all over was what he ultimately wanted. Starting anew was a good first step in that direction.

A minute later, she dropped a bottle of beer in front of him. Swirls of condensation rimmed the top, indicating to him the brisk temperature within the glass.

He placed his hand across the countertop when she turned away. "Stay with me a little while."

She glanced at him and then shook her head. "My, that looks bad. You sure you don't want an ice pack?"

"I'll be fine."

"How did you get it, again?"

He snorted, knowing exactly why she was asking. He never replied the first time she inquired. Here she was, unsatisfied with his lack of explanation.

"A guy blindsided me. I wasn't paying attention."

"What? Who was it? Was it here?"

He shook his head. "No."

"But why would he do that?"

"He was trying to rob me."

"Did you call the cops?"

He chuckled. "Didn't have time to wait for them."

She made a small sound. "Oh, I'm so sorry, Weldon. You sure you don't want an ice pack or something?"

Weldon held up the tall glass in front of him. "The cold beer is good. Don't need anything else." *Except for you, beside me, as my mate.* He left the unsaid words dangling in his mind as he took in her gorgeous smile.

"Well, I'm glad you didn't get hurt, you know, worse than you already are."

He slowly shook his head. "I'm not the one that gets hurt."

She eyed him suspiciously. "Speaking of which, I'm going to need to attend to my roommate since you broke her heart."

"She broke mine first."

"Truly?"

"She cheated on me."

Tania slapped her hand across her chest and gasped. "I find that hard to believe."

Weldon's wide grin displayed a set of perfect, white teeth. "Why? Because I'm so good-looking?"

"No. Because you're full of it."

He threw his head back and heartily laughed.

"Seriously, though, I'm sorry she did that to you. Being cheated on hurts."

He slid his fingers across the sleek glass of his beer bottle. "Had experience?"

"Yeah. My last boyfriend. The jerk. Caught him in bed with the cleaning lady."

Weldon's eyebrows drew up. "Really? He didn't deserve you."

She clasped her hands together in front of her as she leaned over the counter. "Yeah. Probably not."

"You deserve much better."

She smirked. "Oh? And you would know that how?"

"I get a sense that you're a good person."

She snorted and then pushed off the bar. "Well, my time here is almost up. I gotta get ready. You take care of yourself, Weldon."

He nodded. "Oh, I'll be back." He shoved off the barstool and threw several bills onto the countertop.

"Thanks." She smiled, picking up the tip before she walked to the other end of the counter, whipping off the black apron and ditching it behind the bar. He watched her stroll away, grateful they were in a better place than they'd been earlier in the day.

WELDON ROLLED UP HIS window as he neared his destination. After almost eleven hours on the road, he knew he had to find a place to rest for the night. Perfect and convenient with its fast-food restaurants, shower stalls, and bathroom facilities, the nearby truck stop was just the thing. Normally, he'd pay for a hotel room. This time, with having cut it close with delivery hours plus surviving an extended time waiting for the massive breakdown on the interstate to clear up, he figured he didn't have the extra time to seek a nearby hotel. A rebel by nature, if he truly wanted to spend the night in a hotel bed, he would. Tonight, he craved the open air, the trees beyond the facility, and the majestic night scenery versus four walls and noisy neighbors.

Parking his rig into an allocated parking spot for tractor-trailer vehicles, he stepped down from the running board to begin the post-trip inspection. Several minutes later, he flipped through pages on his clipboard and started checking the lights when an unusual sound piqued his interest. Turning his head toward its origin, he found a scrawny-looking, tall woman descending from a truck opposite from where he stood. One look at her informed him what she was.

He hadn't seen many lot lizards in his travels. Therefore, her presence surprised him. He could be wrong about her. Yet, the fact that her strong stench, rushing his nostrils, had him gagging in the middle of his checklist only confirmed the likelihood of his suspicion. She had, recently, been with someone, possibly the truck driver beginning his own post-trip inspection of his vehicle. The way she dashed toward the front door of the convenience store, eyeballing men along the way, indicated she was ready for her next customer.

Weldon shook his head as he worked on completing his list. He'd never been with a lot of lizard before. He'd never been that desperate. Knowing their lifestyle and reading several fantastical stories on trucking websites, he knew the pros and cons. There was only one pro. Getting your rocks off when you truly needed it, quickly and efficiently. Weldon never had that problem.

He wasn't boastful when he said women fell over themselves when he was around. They did. Weldon casually sat back and watched them present their wares to him. It was akin to sales representatives presenting services, hoping he'd choose one of them for the night. When he wanted a warm body in his cold bed, he'd take one home. On a few occasions, he indulged in threesomes, bringing two women home at a time with him. Yet that was during his younger days when he was a young pup. For the last few decades, he'd opted for one-on-one entertainment instead. Yet that would all stop once he claimed Tania. Once she was his, there'd be no others for either of them.

An image of Tania's porcelain skin and sharp features twirled swirls of pleasure straight through his system, effectively tenting the front of his pants. If the lot lizard was here right now to witness his excitement. —Thank goodness she was still inside the store, drumming up business. Weldon had no interest in her, anyway.

His eyebrows drew together with the strange jingle chiming from his phone. Who would be calling him at this hour? He had no girlfriend, and he had since changed his phone number to thwart his past bedmates' attempts to negotiate another opportunity in the sack. Was it, instead, Kingsley calling him, or more likely, the company he contracted with for his current delivery? Maybe they had another assignment waiting for him back home? He released the phone from the clip holding it in place and glanced at the screen before swiping right to allow the call to come through.

"Hey. You caught me at a bad time. Is everything okay?"

A deceptively honey-sweet tone of voice riddled with sarcasm welcomed him. "Oh? When is a good time for you?"

He glanced at the screen again. Almost certain Kara had called him and not Tania. Besides, they had never exchanged numbers.

"Is this Tania?"

"Who else would it be? Or do you have a string of girlfriends you're waiting to hear from? I'll wait if you have to grab another line."

He rumbled a low chuckle. "Who's being the smartass now?" If only Tania was beside him, he'd gladly throw her over his knee and punish that plump ass of hers till she begged for mercy. From what little he knew of her, he'd bet she wouldn't take the discipline, easily, without a fight. *Oh, please resist*, he silently begged. *Please*. The repercussions would prove exciting and rewarding.

"Kara wants you to pick up your stuff. She has it all neatly packed up in the living room. And she wants her key back."

Her key? Oh hell. He smacked the back of his hand across his forehead. He forgot he had a key. He had insisted he didn't need one and that they were only dating, but Kara wouldn't listen. Wanting him back permanently, she gave him a key to try to solidify something with him despite his resistance to accept it. He'd gladly give her back the item he never wanted in the first place but running into her to claim his items didn't seem like a good idea. What if she begged him to come back, once again? In front of Tania? He couldn't, very well, shout expletives at her and then walk away, dragging his belongings behind him.

"Hello? Did you hear me? Kara wants your stuff out of our place."

Why don't you just move them into your room? I am your mate, after all. Weldon left the unspoken words hanging in the air between them.

"I'm in Anchorage right now. I'll pick them up when I get back."

She snorted. "Anchorage? Okay. So, when will that be?"

He spoke through gritted teeth. "None of your business."

"Oh yeah? Well,, Kara's my roommate and now, my friend, so yes, it *is* my business to know when she will have peace of mind, away from you. Maybe I should just haul your stuff to your placc and then dump it all outside of your door and let any passerby at them? What do you think about that?"

Weldon couldn't help the smile forming across his lips. The woman had spunk. He loved that in a female.

"I'll be back in a few days. If it's not too much for Kara to hold onto my stuff till then."

"Listen, bub, we are not a storage facility. Come pick up your stuff and soon." She promptly ended the call.

"Thanks for calling." He sneered amidst dead air before sliding the phone underneath the clip attached to his belt.

Damn, the woman was frustrating. She was gorgeous, beyond compare and provocative as hell, yet stubborn and demanding, too. Despite the tense, uneasy feeling she aroused in him, he wanted her. All of her.

He dropped the clipboard onto the driver's seat, grabbed his jacket, and slammed the door. Weldon's stomach gurgled in agreement as he aimed toward the fast-food restaurants attached to the convenience store. His choices ended up fried chicken or burgers. He chose the latter, less greasy alternative, informing a cute, flirty cashier of his choice and adding a large side of fries and a soda to his order. She gave him a wide smile as she cashed him out. He drew in her scent, remarking to himself the difference between her and Tania. Tania had a pungent though delectable flavor his beast craved. He would happily bathe in her scent any day- every day if she let him. This young twenty-something year old's aroma was lighter, sweeter, and as innocent as her blue-colored doe eyes conveyed to the world. Barely touched by men, she hungered for experiences. The way she kept glancing at Weldon, the heat of her excitement teasing him from behind the counter, told him more than she knew. She wanted Weldon.

Tapping the bill of his cap in her honor, he promptly dropped into one of two plastic chairs attached to a small, square table and unwrapped the burger. Freeing it from the paper and effectively smothering its delicious contents within the two sesame seed buns, he brought the juicy burger to his lips. Unhinging his jaw, he satisfied his senses with one eager bite. Sauce dribbled to the corners of his mouth and between his fingers. Rivulets of the liquid streamed down his arms as flavor bursts assaulted his tongue, and the spices overwhelmed his nostrils. His fangs threatened to expose themselves, delighting in the meaty taste of his main course. He preferred a different type of food source. Fancying fresh versus cooked. With the addition of a warm, thick liquid coating his raw throat instead of the mottled brown, thin texture from the aluminum can next to him. The burger was certainly a good option when alternatives were unavailable.

The cashier giggled as she approached. He scanned her over. Possibly his preferred liquid refreshment was available, after all. She swabbed a few napkins over the saucy mess across his forearms.

She chided, "My, you really like your burgers." Scrunching the napkins into tight balls in the palm of her hand, she slipped into the seat across from him.

Weldon looked up at her in between bites. "Shouldn't you be working?"

"I'm on break. So, what are you doing around these parts? I've never seen you here before. "

"I had a delivery from Fairbanks."

"You delivered from there to Anchorage? Cool. You must drive one of those big trucks?"

He lifted an amused eyebrow. " Tractor-trailer? Yeah."

"Can I see it? I've never been in one before."

He swallowed a large morsel of meat, previously stuck in the back of his throat. "Aren't you a bit young?"

She shrugged her shoulders. "I'm twenty-two and unattached. I think you're handsome. Why? You got a girl somewhere?"

Yeah. He did. But she wasn't here. Still, if he was in a solid, defined relationship with Tania, he'd never consider an alternative. This waif was giving him ideas.

"Meet me at my truck in an hour if you can. I'll give you a tour." Weldon cleared his throat, urging the tightening between his thighs to simmer down. Images of taking the blonde on her back, on all fours, and then on his lap urged him to drop his meal and run back to the truck, immediately, to satiate his hunger. He pointed to his truck in the parking lot as she winked and walked away. He couldn't wait to get her inside the cab and maybe the trailer. He'd lay a blanket across the trailer's floor, so she'd remain comfortable while he took them to heaven and back.

The anticipation of lying with her almost kept him from finishing his meal. Yet, he knew he needed the strength and energy to keep up with her youth. He scarfed down the remainder of his fries and took several swigs of his soda when he spotted the lot lizard slinking up to a table next to him. She eyed him in between words to her next victim. When the guy passed on her offer, she snuck up to Weldon's table and stumbled out a sentence. Her bloodshot eyes peered over at him beneath heavy eyelids.

"Hey stud, you looking for some fun?"

He grimaced as her pungent odor attacked his nostrils. "Not with you. No."

"Well damn. You don't have to be so mean."

He waved her away. "Move on to another. You'll get nothing from me."

She spat at him before she sauntered off. "You are some asshole, you know."

He chuckled to himself as he watched her slide into a seat opposite of a bearded man. Yeah, he knew it all right. He never pretended to be anything other than what he was. He stood up, threw out the remaining contents on his tray, and then sought out the cashier, giving her a nod as he caught her gaze. It was time to get his truck and himself ready for her visit.

Chapter Five

Weldon's heart hurt. He hadn't expected to feel any pain from his acts with the young damsel lying next to him. Granted, he still didn't know her name, but it didn't matter, for he'd never see her again. Yet, the fact that anything inside of him felt off or with discord was beyond his comprehension. They'd just engaged in several mind-blowing, fantastical sex acts he never knew possible. The girl was incredibly flexible. He was able to take her in positions he physically couldn't with other females. It was the advantage of youth. Still, it made for an unimaginable, amazing experience he'd never forget.

During their fourth joining, he couldn't help himself. He yearned for a nibble, and, as a result, his one fang protruded. Her irises captured sudden distress when she caught the fang lingering a bit too low outside of his mouth. Her own mouth opened wide, threatening to expose him. He slammed his hand over her lips before she wailed and then stared straight into her eyes, calming her with specific words before he released her. She relaxed under him, jutting her neck toward him to tease him, and offering him the very essence his secondary beast craved. The more he focused on the blood beating within her very veins, the less restraint he had. He was a goner. He had to have her.

He leaned forward, drawing in her scent for a brief moment before opening his jaw. His incisors lengthened and sliced through her thin flesh. He grunted in recognition and indulgence of his basal pleasure flooding through his awareness as his body gave in to the carnal desire it sought. Her blood gushed up at him like lava from a volcano. It coated the inside of his mouth and saturated his throat, slipping down to his stomach. He siphoned every drop he was able to without rendering her unconscious or, worse, dead. Grunting and relishing in the raw liquid refreshment that fed his very soul, he snuck a peek at her face. He found her eyes wide open, frozen in an expression he couldn't see. She said nothing. Did nothing to deter him. Staying perfectly still and motionless, allowing the animal within him to bask in her lifeforce—a gift she unconsciously granted him.

When he was done, he ripped her from his grasp, dropping her lighter weight onto the blanket while he wiped his mouth with the back of his hand. Licking his lips to his guttural sound of gratification, he sucked on his knuckles, lapping up the fine juices that spilled across his arm. He wasn't wasting a drop. Finished, he plopped down beside her. Regretting that he had to accept her bonus offer in the back of a cold, fifty-three-foot trailer instead of his comfortable, discreet King-sized bed, clouding his mind. He took less than a minute to lock her gaze and command her to forget his indulgence of her liquid assets. He smoothed his fingers over the two puncture marks in her neck and watched them heal into non-existence. Then he rolled back onto the blanket, images of Tania intruding and reminding him his heart belonged to another.

He heard sniffles then the beginning of small sobs. The girl was crying and mumbling in between her tears something about the best sex she ever had. Weldon smiled. He knew he was good but damn. She was definitely inexperienced. Holding her in his arms, he pushed her out of his mind, imagining Tania. Every expression, every bit of exploring and teasing he did was on Tania's body, not hers. He took Tania four times, and it was the best sex he ever had, but it wasn't real. Tania wasn't here. The fact urged him to blubber beside the waif, crying out for his mate- the only woman he truly wanted.

The girl dried her eyes and snuggled next to him in the length of the air-conditioned trailer. He allowed it, only wanting the female suddenly transformed into his true love instead of a one-night stand. He'd been horny. He thought lying with her would satiate him, but it didn't. The desire to toss the girl aside, jump into the driver's seat of his rig and take off to find Tania overwhelmed his insides. Yet, the relationship with Tania was only starting to blossom. They were nowhere near bedmates and not even friends yet.

He yearned for more with Tania, but he knew he had to remain patient. Getting Tania was going to take some time, for she was untrusting and wary of men. He sensed this from her from the start. Still, he wanted her. He knew he'd have her in the end. They were fated to be together. Yet, claiming her heart wasn't going to be easy. She wouldn't just walk up to him and ask to be taken. Not like the girl beside him had. The idea of Tania's mouth forming the words he wanted to hear enlivened his insides and woke up the lengthening leviathan between his thighs. The girl stirred and smiled.

She folded her fingers around his length and softly squeezed. "I see someone's awake." He brushed her hand off and turned away from her.

He wasn't interested in a fifth-round- with her. Glancing at his watch, he lifted off the blanket and looked at her. "It's four a.m. I gotta get ready to go." He gazed at her, taking one last look at her small breasts, her firm stomach, and her tight derriere. He helped her up and then picked up the blanket. She quickly dressed while he threw on a pair of jeans. Assisting her out the tailgate, he thanked her for a good time. When she offered her number, he shook his head.

Running the back of his fingers down one cheek, he gave her a quick peck on the lips and spoke. "You should concentrate on school. Stay away from the bad boys and find a good man, later —" He paused, waiting for her to say her name, for he still didn't know it. He'd like to remember her during those long, cold nights when the entwined beasts within him pined for their mate.

"Ashley."

He repeated her name, offering his in return.

The sweet innocence glazing over her eyes called to something buried deep within him. "If you're in the area, maybe we can hook up again?"

"Maybe," he offered, brushing his hand across her cheek. He stepped around the corner and walked toward the driver's side door. "You take care of yourself, Ashley. —and —thank you." It was only right to express gratitude for allowing him, a stranger, to delight in her bounteous liquid confection. Giving such a gift freely to him wasn't something he expected or naturally experienced from a human. He considered coming back for the waif if Tania rejected him. Ashley would never be his mate, but she'd make a good second. Inexperienced and craving adventure, he'd happily fulfill both of her needs while satisfying his wolf's urge to protect and procreate.

Yet, he couldn't process that now. He had a mission as soon as he stepped back in Fairbanks. He had to grab his stuff and somehow avoid Kara's presence and Tania's judgment. He stepped up into the driver's seat, grabbed his logbook, and started the pre-trip inspection checklist before he started the long drive back home.

THE MUSICAL LULLABY pouring out of the female's mouth played at his heartstrings. "Who is it?"

Instead of responding with words, he whined. His legs threatened to buckle beneath him. He grabbed onto the door handle as simultaneously the door was opened, and he fell flat on his face.

A female figure fell to her knees, next to him. Her hand touched his shoulder. "Oh my God, are you okay?"

He grunted seconds before inhaling. Then he groaned as Tania's magical scent invaded his nostrils and rushed his internal organs, ensnaring each within a perpetual state of bliss. Why in the hell did she have to be home?

Tania giggled. "We have to stop meeting this way." He pushed off the floor, standing when she continued. "Are you sure you're okay?"

Gritting his teeth with the continuous assault of her mouth-watering perfume to his system, he grabbed onto the wall and propelled himself past the apartment door.

"You look like you're in pain. Do you want an ice pack or an aspirin?"

"I'm just here to grab my stuff."

"I know that, but I don't want you walking around injured. You could sue us."

He snapped his neck toward her and caught her teasing smile. She was only kidding.

"That was a good one," he said, limping his way over to their sofa. "Maybe I'll just sit a minute and then go." He fell back into the cushions and then asked, "Is Kara here?"

Tania shook her head in response. "She got your voicemail about coming over. She took off an hour ago."

He swallowed back the dry lump forming in his throat. The last thing he wanted was to make an enemy. "Is she okay?"

Tania twisted her lips into a sexy semi-pout. "What do you think?"

Weldon hunched his shoulders over his lap and leaned forward. Glancing at the ground, he muttered, "No. I suppose she isn't." Drawing in a strong whiff of her scent, he growled out, "If I had your number, I wouldn't have had to bother her."

"Oh no. You'll have to do a hell of a lot more than that to get my number. Besides, I don't date leftovers." Tania pushed up from the sofa's arm and pointed at two boxes to the left of the front door. "Your stuff is over there when you're ready."

"Don't date leftovers, huh? What if I had a real interest in you?"

Tania laughed aloud. "Don't press your luck, sailor. I plan to remain single forever."

"Forever, eh? That's a really long time to predict anything from now."

"Oh no. I'm sure of it. I've dated too many losers. All of them failed me in one way or another. I'm done with looking for Mr. Right. I'm not looking for long-term with anyone anymore."

He grabbed ahold of his chest, surprised at the sudden, intense pain he was feeling inside. Her words literally stung him. She rushed over to him as he wavered close to falling off the edge of the sofa.

She pushed him back toward the cushions, keeping him upright. "You need help."

No. I need you. The unspoken words remained hanging between them. "What if I told you I was heartbroken by your words?"

She twisted her head to one side and stared at him. "I can't figure you out. Why are you still here?"

The urge to make a bold move overrode his intellectual brain. "Because I like you." As soon as he said the words, he wanted to retrieve them, especially when he caught the look on her face.

She covered her mouth and laughed, doubling over with giggles and snorts in the end.

Weldon shot up from the couch. He briskly walked around her form, previously huddling in front of him. "Never mind what I said. I'll just go grab my stuff and leave you alone." He lifted both boxes with little effort and started for the door.

"Wait." Her single word stopped him. The surprised look on her face made him turn around. "You're serious? You really like me? But you barely know me."

He shrugged his shoulders and re-positioned the boxes in his hands. "I like what I like."

Tania rushed past him. "Here, let me help you." She turned the doorknob and opened the door for him, stopping him as he crossed the threshold. "I can't date you, you know. You're my roommate's ex."

"I know."

Weldon took one last wistful sniff of her, stepped onto the breezeway, and then walked away.

KINGSLEY SHOT AROUND a tree but missed him. Weldon pushed harder, filling his lungs with impossibly more air before shooting off and running as fast as he could. He expended every ounce of energy and frustration through his strong limbs until he could barely breathe. Leaping over a small mound, he fell onto the ground and yelped, knowing he bruised something internally if not sprained something. He didn't care. He deserved it. Tania would never be his. Kingsley skidded to a stop, nosing him in the chest and growling, "Tag, you're it," before rushing into the woods.

Weldon lifted to a stand, stretching his front legs and then his back before shaking the dirt off his reddish-brown fur. He started at a trot, searching for Kingsley among the tall trees and thick bushes lining the wild outdoors that was their playground. When he sensed his energy reserve was replenished, he broke into a run.

A shrill sound pierced the air. Weldon spotted Kingsley forming a wide arc in front of him instead of running straight and escaping Weldon's detection. With a quick U-turn, Kingsley ran past him, barking at him as he approached. The sound echoed once again, and this time Weldon caught it. It was Eva.

"Boys. Dinner's ready," she called from the porch.

As Eva was Kingsley's mate, it made sense that he heard her call first. If Weldon could only shut down the sound of Tania's voice, he might have some peace. At least, out in the wild, the chances of finding Tania out here were slim to none. As long as he stayed away from the places she frequented, he'd eventually get over her. He chuffed in the middle of his panting. If it was only that easy. Wolves mated for life. Tania's rejection damned him to an uncertain, unhappy future.

"There you are." Kingsley ran straight into Eva's open arms, barreling her over with his force. She giggled as she fell backward. He hovered over her, showering her with kisses, licking over parts of her upper torso while remaining in wolf form. Weldon looked on, a wistful sensation clouding over his eyes and weighing heavily upon his heart. At no point in his life did he envy anything Kingsley had, but today, he craved a loving relationship like Kingsley had with Eva. Since they met, the two were fascinated with each other, never getting enough of each other's company. Weldon wanted the same kind of relationship. Someone he could fawn over, protect, and enjoy precious moments with.

At one hundred and eighty-five years old, he wasn't getting any younger. Without a love interest- or a distraction to keep him sane, the years ahead of him threatened to pass by morbidly slow. He'd give Tania another chance. If she rejected him a second time, he'd move on to, hopefully, greener fields and his choice of available women. He'd choose one to reign as his queen. Although the idea of leaving Tania a distant memory threatened his aching heart to shatter completely into shards of irreparable pieces, Weldon wouldn't give up. Doing so proved too painful.

"YOU MEAN TAPPER?" TANIA'S co-worker and friend, RJ, asked.

Tania finished drying off a glass and then started on another. "What are you talking about?"

"Tapper. We call him Tapper because he has one-night stands. You know. He taps you, and then he's gone."

Tania snapped her mouth shut with the surprising news. Shuffling past multitudes of ideas swirling through her head, she couldn't come up with a good response. She focused on drying the glass in her hand. Then moved on to the dozens more on the counter, waiting for her.

RJ angled her head to one side. Worry lines etched across her forehead as her bushy eyebrows dipped toward each other, almost forming into one long line. "Are you okay? You didn't know. —Did I burst your bubble?" She laughed.

Tania grimaced. "No. I didn't think he was loyal. At least not outside of a relationship. He was dating my roommate. She was the one that cheated."

RJ gasped. "You don't say. Tapper was cheated on by one of his ladies. Wow. Talk about karma."

Tania brought the glass she was working on up to the lights shining brightly above the bar. She nodded her approval and then placed it back down, grabbing another one and repeating the process all over again. She ignored her female counterpart's continued stare, knowing she wanted a reply but finding nothing to say in response to all she learned about Weldon. It wasn't

Tania's place to have an opinion about him anyway. She didn't, personally, know him. Still, she knew most men were like Weldon. That's why she didn't date anymore.

Her last boyfriend- or should she say, fiancée'- handed her a prenup, a maneuver she never thought she'd experience. Having nothing against prenups, in general, still, she thought she'd end up the last person in the world to ever have one-handed to her. Boy, was she wrong? The cold paperwork in front of her left her with a similar frigid feeling inside. As much as she didn't want the simple words on the paper to affect her decision to spend forever with the man she figured she loved, it did. Refusing to sign the form, he left her shortly afterward. She recalled the moment-by-moment details that wrenched her heart into two. She could've sworn they meant more to each other. Yet, he was too concerned with keeping his assets safe- her not being one of the assets he expected to claim for himself.

She recalled his adamant frown and the disgusting words he tossed at her before he retrieved the form and stormed for the front door. She grabbed at her chest at the memory of the intense pain that held her insides ransom. She had watched the sexy, strong back and muscled physique of the man she had hoped to marry slam the door behind him. That finality forever shut down any notion of getting back together. To think, their year-long relationship suddenly ended- all because she wouldn't sign a piece of paper.

Although he had money, it wasn't the reason she was marrying him. The fact was, she couldn't get past the idea of the paperwork hanging over her head. It didn't sit well with her, and the idea of a prenup felt wrong and uncomfortable, churning up unwanted acid in her stomach. Yet, he wouldn't hear her out. He directed her to sign the form, or they wouldn't move forward. After he walked out of her life, she dated a few others, though never with serious intent. The idea of finding a suitable match crumbled with her fiancée's footsteps out her door. He was her only fiancée. She was sure he was the one. He crumpled her dreams of sharing the rest of her life with a wondrous life partner and tossed them straight into a wastebasket the day he left.

Still, when she met Weldon, something inside her changed. She couldn't dismiss the fact that the man was unbelievably handsome. With a six-pack for abs and firm muscles every-where else, he invaded her dreams at several points since they met. She licked her lips as she rubbed out a smudge from the outer corner of the glass. The man was an incredible tempta-tion her brain warned her against indulging in. Sadly, her girl parts didn't care to listen.

Although their first meeting ended up an unsavory ex-change of words, Weldon made an impression on her she wouldn't soon forget. Anytime he appeared, she found it dif-ficult to tamp down the sudden racing of her heart or ignore the tantalizing smell of his manly, musky scent. And when he spoke to her in that growly voice. —She swallowed a sudden dry lump in her throat and caught R J's Cheshire cat grin.

"You like him, don't you?"

Tania rubbed the glass in her hand a bit too hard. She read-justed her grip when it almost rolled off her palm, heading to-ward the tile floor. "What? No. Of course not."

"It's okay. I think most of the girls here have had their fun with him. He's good for a roll in the hay for one or two days but be forewarned, Tapper doesn't do permanent, with anyone."

Tania dropped the glass onto the countertop and threw the bar towel onto the counter with an exasperated sigh. "I'm not interested." Tania moved to the end of the counter, turning away from RJ to mask her confused emotions. If RJ snuck a peek at her right now, she'd know she was lying. Tania was almost certain RJ knew that fact, anyway, without having to glance at her.

Why was Weldon like all the others? Why couldn't he be different?

Chapter Six

Ties, cords, bondage? Tania didn't know what it was called. —Still, something about Weldon drew her to him. She only wished she could sever, permanently, the intense urge to act on her emotions and jump the man's bones already. She couldn't help the excitement she felt any time he was near. Now that she knew he was a womanizer, she'd have to try harder to stay out of his grasp. The task was proving difficult the more frequently he showed up at her place of work. Strangely enough, he seemed to pop into the bar most nights she was on shift.

Still, she'd had her share of carousing, cheating bastards. She wasn't about to add another one to her long list of losers.

Speaking of which—

"Hi, beautiful."

Damn. There he was again with the insincere compliments. She welcomed them before, but now that she knew what he was- a wolf in sheep's clothing- no thanks. She'd rather face the wolf and fend for herself.

"What do you want?" She hissed at the harsh tone and words that whirled out of her mouth before she had a chance to press edit.

"Hard night?"

She tapped her fingernails beneath the countertop. Impatience fueling her veins, she was ready to move on to another subject or another customer should one show up. "Maybe."

"Let me buy you a drink."

"I'm on the clock."

"Afterward."

Smooth. Real smooth. She wasn't falling for his cock and bullshit. Not now.

"I see you found him." Tania jerked with the whisper over her shoulder. How in the world did RJ sneak up behind her without her notice? Weldon smiled as RJ wiggled by.

A stab of jealousy zinged her in the gut.

"RJ can serve you if you need time to make up your mind. I have work to do."

He uttered her name in that sexy, growly voice. She stopped in her tracks and turned toward Weldon.

"Tell me what's wrong."

"Why? We never talk." She realized her error when he raised his eyebrows. "I mean, we talk but about nothing serious."

"I can be your confidant."

She scoffed.

"I'm serious. Try me."

"Why?"

Weldon offered. "I want to be your friend."

"I hate to repeat myself again, but why?"

The corners of his lips curled up into a smile. "Because I like you."

"Yeah. Me and every other girl you meet." She murmured under her breath. "Tapper liking me. Hilarious."

"I see they've been talking about me."

She slammed her hand over her mouth and caught his toothy grin. She shook her head. "I'm sorry. I didn't mean —"

"Yeah, you did." He shrugged his shoulders. "I don't care."

"How does it not bother you? What others say about you."

He slid off the barstool and positioned himself at the end of the counter, smiling at her as he spoke. "Other people's opinions don't matter." He grabbed her arm as she started to swing toward the dining room, making her escape. "Except yours."

His gaze latched onto hers. They stared at each other for several long seconds before he continued. "I don't want you to think badly of me. If you did, I'd regret every bit of gossip that was true."

She scrunched her eyebrows together in a puzzled look. "You're a strange one, Weldon. I still don't understand you. Maybe I never will."

"Let's talk. When do you get off work?"

"Actually, tonight's an early day for me. I'm here for another forty-five minutes or so."

"I'll come back. Okay?" He tilted her chin up to meet his eyes.

She attempted to ignore the butterflies in her stomach reviving at his single touch. She spoke, silently chastising herself at the meek tone of her voice. "Yes." Her knees trembled and threatened to buckle beneath her. Damn, if the man didn't affect all her parts —

He gave her a victorious smile. "I'll be back. Don't you dare leave before I show up. I'll track you down if I have to."

She watched him strut confidently out the door, her gaze dropping down his long, lean back and across his firm butt cheeks. What in the hell was she doing? She should've said no.

A BEAM OF SUNLIGHT washed across her closed eyelids, teasing her into waking. She lifted one arm in the air, overhead, and then the other while yawning loudly and stretching her toes beneath the sheets. She smiled as she sunk back into the softness cradling her. Never getting enough hours of sleep last night proved different. She could've sworn it was the best, most relaxing sleep of her life. She even dreamt of a certain cavalier, naked and on top of her. The scandalous things they did in dreamland had heat rushing to her cheeks and another, not unpleasant sensation flooding her nether regions. If he was here, she'd beg for round two. Yet, first, he'd have to repeat with her what he did last night. Not many men went downtown and enjoyed it. Yet, Weldon did.

Of course, Weldon had tons of experience, bedding all the women in town. After all of the gals he ended up with, one would assume he'd prove talented in bed. Tania couldn't argue. Weldon was a skilled professional.

Tania's eyelids popped open with the warm hand sliding across her hip. She jerked left and saw him. Oh God, no! What in the hell did she do last night? She grimaced as a vivid picture of the two of them entwined popped into her brain. Oh hell. She had divulged too much to Weldon last night. Told him things she never told anyone else. She even let it slip that she found him attractive, and now here she was, another notch on his bedpost. Damn. What more could go wrong?

Carefully, she lifted his arm off her hip and scooted beneath it. She inched her way off the side of the bed, holding her breath and trying not to jar him awake with her movements. Finally, like a runner jumping the hurdles, she leaped off the edge of the bed. Landing on her toes, she fell back on her heels with her hands triumphantly in the air in a "ta-da" show of victory. Tiptoeing around the bed, she watched Weldon, checking for signs he was awake or near it.

Clamoring for her clothes, she checked her surroundings and figured she was at his place, wherever that was. How could she go to bed with someone she hardly knew and —a womanizer, to boot? Shame on her. Never mind that it was the best sex she ever had. According to RJ, he didn't do *permanent*. They called him Tapper for a reason.

She mumbled under her breath as she dressed in the living room. "That was a stupid move, T." She really had to pee, but there was no way she was searching the premises for a bathroom. Not with him naked in the bed, ready to awaken at any moment. She took one last long look at the handsome devil that gave her the most amazing night to remember and then booked it, scampering toward the door to her freedom. She gripped the door handle and gently pried it open. Careful to slip out without an incident, a loud "ding-ding" sounded, jarring her enough to screech her disagreement with the noise.

Without another thought, she skipped out the door. She slammed it behind her, the loud tone of Weldon's voice growing closer and urging her to scamper out to her car and away from him as quickly as possible. Slapping a hand across the side of her head, she shoved dark glasses over her eyes. She whimpered all the way to the car, the pounding headache from her hangover rudely welcoming her to start her day before she wanted to.

Weldon shouted her name several times, and she ignored each one, her hands trembling over her keys as she fought to find the key fob to open the driver's side door. Dressed in only a black robe, he almost caught up to her when she slid behind the steering wheel, locked the door, and pressed the start button for the ignition. Her heart raced as he pounded on her glass. She caught the questioning look across his face, which under normal circumstances might've melted her heart and changed her mind about leaving. Instead, she shifted the car into drive and pressed down on the gas pedal, only daring to breathe when his condo was no longer in view in her rearview mirror.

After several minutes, her panicked breaths slowed, and her heartbeat returned to normal. Images of Weldon intruded. As he pounded on her glass to get her attention, he looked sad, confused, and surprised at what she was doing. Tania hated to witness his disappointment. Last night was—unexpected but beautiful. If he wasn't such a rake, she would've thought it meant something to him. Yet, she knew better.

Tania swiped at tears forming in the corners of her eyes. Weldon was an amazing lover. He said things to her last night she never heard from anyone else. He made her feel special and appreciated like she was some prize or treasure to be cherished. No man ever made her feel that way before. Yet, Weldon had a way with women. It was likely why the women who bedded him wanted him in the first place. His charisma and charm drew them to his bed like something drew Tania to him last night.

She stared at her phone as it sounded at a stoplight. Turning it over, she laid it on the passenger seat and glanced at the screen. It was Weldon. How did he get her number? Oh yeah —they exchanged numbers last night to start a friendship. What a joke. Their effort to start something ended things quickly, instead. At least they enjoyed some fireworks before the inevitable explosion.

There was no way in hell she'd return his calls. She had to process what happened and what to do next. Bedding a customer was normal, but a customer she had a real interest in —That was forbidden. She grabbed the phone between Weldon's attempts to contact her and called the bar. She was taking the rest of the week off.

WHAT HAPPENED? THAT'S what Weldon wanted to know. One minute they were having fun. Laughing, chatting, and opening up to each other—the next, they ended up in bed, mutually satisfying each other to a gratifying, explosive finish. Tania was experienced, but that didn't matter to Weldon, who had more than his share of women. He wanted Tania to be his last. He was working his way to making that happen when she ditched him this morning. Was last night that awful? It was the best sex he ever had with anyone. At least, in his opinion. Of course, he never cared for the other women he bedded. They were only amusement. Yet, Tania- she was his future.

If they had a great time, why did she bolt? Maybe he didn't measure up? He growled. That couldn't be the answer. She had no complaints and only compliments last night when she shouted his name several times. Did he not give her what she needed? Visions of her raking her fingernails down his back and screaming for joy intruded. Definitely not the answer, either. Then what was it? He was about to solidify their relationship this morning, making sure she knew she was his girlfriend. She accelerated out of his place so fast he hadn't a chance to say much of anything except for roaring her name out in frustration.

He flung his phone down onto the dinner table. Could she be any more infuriating? Now she wasn't answering the phone. He was reluctant to leave any more phone messages after his last one.

"Damn it, Tania. Where are you, and what are you doing? Why are you not picking up the phone? And why did you leave? I need to talk to you, please. Call me."

He stared at the phone, willing the instrument to ring. Instead, it mocked him and remained silent.

He sat down on a nearby chair and leaned over, his elbows resting against his thighs. Scrubbing one hand through his hair, he contemplated what to do. Last night was perfect. Tania was more than he could've hoped for in a mate. She was splendid. She was beautiful. Just her smile did things to his insides he couldn't begin to describe. Why did she leave him? What could he do to make it up to her? How could he tell her how much she meant to him? Especially when she wouldn't pick up the damn phone. He growled, grabbed the phone, and threw it against the wall. Thank goodness it was surrounded by layers of protection, according to the manufacturer that sold him the casing marketed to be water-resistant, shock-resistant, and drop-resistant. Right now, he didn't care if the cellphone shattered into a gazillion microscopic pieces, but he would if she dared to call him back and the useless device didn't work.

Tension welled up within him, flooding through his muscles, constricting them and, ultimately, tightening his jaw. His legs trembled with the need to run- either toward her or through the dense forest, burning up excess energy. The cardio would do his wolf good and allow his human side to think things through. Despite the blaring sun scorching through the lightweight curtains of his living room, he had several spots he could roam unnoticed and beyond the human eye. Weldon reclaimed his cellphone, slipped on a pair of shoes, and grabbed his keys. Although he might garner several looks driving around in his bathrobe, at least it was better than being naked, which is what he'd end up doing once he shifted.

"I NEED YOUR HELP."

Eva stared at Weldon, her mouth agape with curiosity and partial shock. Weldon's question hung in the air between them. What in the hell did a wolf shifter need from her? Maybe her Wiccan powers? Yet, she was still learning. One could say she was in basic training with her lack of skills. Truly, if he needed a witch, he'd be better off contacting her friends for assistance.

"And what do you need from me?"

He scratched his head and shuffled his feet. "You're a woman, right?"

Seriously? Was he unaware of his brother's preferred sexual orientation?

She chuckled. "Last time I checked." Weldon didn't join in the revelry. Instead, his youthful face tightened while deep lines etched across his forehead. His features were constrained with confusion and something else she'd never figure she'd find on the rebellious shifter: worry. What bugged him to the breaking point where he sought her advice?

She dropped the dish she was drying into the dry rack and folded the towel over the stove's handle. "What is it? Are you okay? Should I get Kingsley?"

Weldon's hand shot out in front of him. He shouted, "No! Don't bring him into this. I only want to speak with you."

She indicated a barstool beside him. "Well then, take a seat. Talk."

He scrubbed a hand through his full head of hair. "You see, there's a woman—"

She nodded, a teasing tone to her voice. "Oh—I see your dilemma."

"I'm serious, Eva. I like her—but she ran away from me."

Eva slapped a hand over her mouth, her laughter filling the tiny room regardless of her efforts to stifle her amusement. "I'm sorry, Weldon. I probably shouldn't be laughing at your situation even though I'm sure you did something to warrant her leaving."

"Why would you say that?"

"Have you looked at yourself in the mirror lately? Gentleman isn't a word I'd use to describe you."

He sighed and shook his head. "I know I'm a cad. I've never cared before what anyone thought of me, but she's different. I don't want her to walk away from me. I need her."

Eva tilted her head to one side and eyed him. "Why? You've walked away from every woman before now. Hell,

Kingsley says you're known for warming beds and not staying, and you know it, too. What's different about her?"

"She's my mate."

Eva gasped yet remained silent. Her eyebrows arched up, and her mouth gaped open while she stared at him, attempting to comprehend what he just told her. She blinked her eyes and then blinked again, the jarring notion of Weldon needing anyone sinking slowly into her awareness. The woman who caught his attention must've been a saint. Eva guessed at what she looked like, creating white wings and a halo on the profile of a cover model in her mind. Whoever she was, a round of applause was warranted for catching a roving Romeo like Weldon.

She whipped her head toward a familiar tone of voice and smiled. "What are you two up to?" Eva patted the empty barstool next to her and inched over to accommodate Kingsley's broader girth. He rumbled a satisfied tone as he slipped his arm around her waist and pulled her back toward him, kissing the top of her head when she laid her face against his firm shoulder. "Now, what were you two talking about?"

Eva piped up, first, cutting off Weldon's chance to mess things up. "Nothing much. Weldon was giving me pointers on my Halloween costume."

"Oh? Not going as, a witch this year?" Kingsley teased, earning himself a swat to his broad chest. He grabbed Eva's hand and kissed across her fingertips. He lowered his tone of voice to a mere whisper. "I could do this all night with you."

She jutted her head toward Weldon. "But Darling, we have company."

Kingsley growled. "He can leave."

Eva turned toward Weldon. "Not without one last thing. What we talked about earlier. Cats like to know what you're thinking. A nice, good, long chat will do you good, too. Cats like to express themselves, but they want to know how their so-called owners feel. They need their independence, too, and their own opinion, but they don't know how to act when they find themselves in an unusual or awkward situation. Know what I mean?" Eva winked, and Weldon nodded in response.

"What is this about cats? Weldon, you thinking of adopting one or something?"

Eva chuckled and strummed her fingers over the stubble lining Kingsley's chin. "No, silly, I'm thinking of getting a cat costume. I'm just telling Weldon what cats like and why I think I'm like one."

Kingsley's smile widened. "A cat, eh? You're giving me ideas."

"Well then, I guess Weldon should leave." Eva stepped off the barstool. "Do you want to take home some leftovers? I can pack some up for you."

"Nah, I'll be fine. Dinner was delicious, as usual, but I better head off." Weldon smoothed down the red bandana covering his head and grabbed his helmet on the way to the front door.

Kingsley called out to Weldon before he stepped past the doorframe and out onto the concrete. "You and I need to take a ride one day."

Weldon nodded. "Sounds like a plan. Eva, thank you." He waved and shut the door behind him.

Kingsley's eyebrows furrowed. "How come he didn't thank me?"

Eva, playfully, tapped the bridge of his nose with her index finger. "Because you didn't do anything."

"Oh yeah?" Kingsley's voice rumbled through his chest. "I can think of a few things I'd like to do with you."

Eva screeched as she pushed out of his arms and scurried down the long hallway with Kingsley following closely. The wide, mischievous grin plastered across his face gave her a devilish sneak peek into what was yet to come.

Chapter Seven

E xactly one week later and Weldon was back. At least that's what RJ told Tania when she spotted him seated at the bar, searching for someone RJ had offered him a beverage, but he declined, asking who staffed the bar that night and then re-fining his question to ask, specifically, when his favorite bar-tender, Tania, would be back at work RJ lightly teased him about her own capabilities of fulfilling the job, instead. Then, she informed Weldon that Tania wouldn't be back for a few more days.

After thanking her, he strutted out the door. His fingers flew across the keyboard of his cellphone. RJ assumed he was texting someone.

Tania snuck out from the back hallway, where she'd been hiding, and held her phone out to prove her theory right.

Back in her bedroom, RJ stretched across Tania's recliner. "Why don't you call him back? The guy has it bad for you."

Tania shook her head. "I can't. He's the tapper, remember. And I got tapped, unfortunately. I'm so embarrassed it hap-pened to me. I didn't even want it."

RJ snorted. "Well, you must've wanted him. No one ends up in his bed without wanting him in some way."

Tania shrugged her shoulders. "He is —so sexy. I guess the alcohol lowered my inhibitions. There's no way I'd jump in bed with him while sober. Not knowing what I know about him. Yet, he seemed so sad that I left. I don't know why he keeps contacting me."

"You should call him and find out."

"I can't. I'm afraid of what I'll do or what I'll agree to just by hearing his voice. His knee-weakening, panty-melting voice. I swear to God, RJ, I don't think he has it bad for me because I have it so much worse for him. It's horrible. I can't be trusted around him. He is the worst possible scenario for me. That night was like the best night ever with any man. I so wish he was different. But you can't trust anything that comes out of his mouth. He just wants more piece of the action, and I can't give it to him, not anymore. I just can't. I have to have some pride left."

RJ lifted to a stand. She wrapped her arms around her friend and tsked lightly in her ear. "Girl, I warned you about him, and here you got yourself all entangled with him." She sighed. "I wish I could take it away so you wouldn't hurt anymore."

"I just can't hope for something that will never be. Still, I don't know why I keep thinking about him. Why do I feel so drawn to him? What's wrong with me? I want to dial his number right now and throw caution and experience to the wind."

RJ grabbed ahold of her phone and raised it high in the air between them. "For safe keeping until you have a clear head again." They both glanced at it when it chimed.

Tania shifted in her task chair, leaning her upper body over the edge of the desk. "Is it Weldon?"

R.J.'s gaze scanned across the screen. "Yup. He wants to talk."

"If I hear his voice, I'll melt. I'll let my guard down. I'll give myself leeway to fantasize." Tania shook her head. "I hate not answering him back, but I can't do it. When it comes to Weldon, I am so weak, somehow. It's horrible. I've never acted this way with anyone before."

"You've got to talk to him sometime."

"I know. I hope to have more guts when I'm at work, though I'm not sure what I'll say."

"Maybe you could move out of town or out of state?"

Tania chortled. "Move because of a stalker? Very funny. It's not like I have to be in witness protection or anything because of my one foolish mistake." RJ joined in her laughter but soon changed the subject. After another hour of cheerful banter and remarks regarding a reality show they enjoyed watching together, they heard a loud noise at the door. Almost simultaneously, they whipped their heads toward the origin of the sound and then turned toward each other with eyebrows lifted and mouths agape.

Tania moved toward the door when she caught a low whimpering noise on the other side. She found it odd when the stranger's breaths changed to panting. It seemed the person was either hot from exertion or having difficulty breathing.

"Tania, it's Weldon. I know you're at home. I need to talk to you." His panting soon changed to a long, low whine when she refused to open the door.

"Tania, please talk to me. Tell me what I did wrong."

Tania looked at the wide-eyed RJ staring back at her from the living room, then drew in a deep breath. Gathering the remnants of her courage, she unlocked the deadbolt and threw the door open. She stared straight into hazel eyes, which seemed to change in color, with the direction of the overhead lighting. Right now, his eye color bordered on an unusual yet striking amber.

Weldon's strained words bounced off her eardrums. "Tania. Can we please talk?"

Tania gazed across the lovely texture of his skin, his tightly drawn mouth, and his smooth, sculptured chin. Normally spotlessly dressed and impeccably groomed, his ruffled hair and wrinkled clothing indicated he'd had a rough time since her departure. The protective barrier she encased her heart in as soon as she opened the door shattered to pieces as soon as she glanced into his forlorn irises. Incredibly, the man was a mess. He deserved, at least, an explanation.

"I'll be right back," she called over her shoulder to Weldon. She swiveled on her heel and headed toward her bedroom. Shuffling past RJ, she grabbed ahold of her hand and shoved her into the bedroom while mumbling under her breath a quick recap of what transpired with Weldon seconds ago. A few minutes later, RJ bade them both goodnight and left.

"So, where do you want to go —to talk, that is," Tania asked.

"My home?" Tania shook her head emphatically. What they did back at his house put them into this mess, to begin with. "There's a park—"

"Okay. Should I meet you there?"

He grabbed ahold of her hand. She gasped with the warm contact of his skin on hers. The skittering of electricity from his touch urged her to be careful with her heart. She, badly, wanted them to work. That was the problem.

"I have my bike."

The urge to touch him overwhelmed her. She reached for his red, paisley bandana, sliding her fingers across the soft material, briefly, before, lovingly, caressing the side of his head. "I know. I see you have your bandana on."

"You want to ride with me?"

She shook her head. "I don't know how."

"Just grab onto me. I'll keep you safe."

She chuckled. "Famous last words."

He tilted her chin up and caught her gaze. "I'd never, intentionally, place you in harm's way. Never."

She nibbled across her lower lip. He seemed serious. She had to give him a chance. "Okay. Please be careful."

He slipped his index finger under her chin, caressing her jawline with the start of a smile. "Always."

She followed him to his bike, a mixture of excitement and apprehension unsettling her previous calm, confidence. She grabbed ahold of her stomach as a bit of nausea threatened to change her plans for the evening. He squeezed her arm in reassurance and introduced her to his most prized possession.

He held his arm out at full length, passing it over the length of the machine. "Here she is. One of the most beautiful things in my life." She had to agree. It was quite breathtaking.

The midnight black color was in stark contrast with the canary yellow of his other means of transportation. The one he whisked her away in, to his apartment, that fatal night more than one week ago. The night they made love. *No.* For him, it was sex. She was sure of it. Yet, for her, his skillful hands excavated something within her, she thought long gone. The need to settle down with the right guy overwhelmed her with the several hours she spent in Weldon's bedroom. That night, she treated him as if he was gold: pure, coveted treasure. What she ultimately wanted from him was permanency, a more endearing romantic relationship and not a casual fling. How she came to that conclusion, as quickly as she did with, ultimately, a stranger, was something she couldn't explain with mere words. It was something she felt in the depth of her soul. Somehow, she and Weldon were drawn to each other. They made sense. There was no way she could explain the craziness behind her conclusion.

There was only one problem. Weldon didn't *do* permanent.

He was an adventurer, a nomad of sorts, and a connoisseur of women. Here he was, strapping on her helmet and assisting her onto the back of his bike. She recalled a book she read a while ago. The women who sat on the back of a man's bike were considered sweeties, aka non-permanent, willing, and wanton women who hoped to make their way up the chain of a motorcycle gang by latching onto one of the men in the group. Of course, there were *old ladies* too, but that term didn't sit well with her, either. She considered what Weldon might call her.

He turned toward her. "Are you comfortable? Put your arms around my waist."

Did she really need to? The less contact she had with his amazing body, the better off she was.

He issued her a warning while revving the engine at the same time. "Tania —"

She slipped her arms around his waist, sighing with the pleasant musky scent of him wafting through her nostrils. Placing her head against the back of his leather jacket, she deeply inhaled while reveling in the comfort and peace of holding onto her man- albeit a short-term man who was taking her to God knows where to supposedly chat. She might end up on her back or on her knees again, instead. If she did, she'd enjoy this one last night of passion before she said goodbye to him, forever.

They rode for quite a while. Tania's arms were welded across Weldon's waist, securing her safety with his movements. Pretty confident he wouldn't do anything wild or crazy on his bike to show off as some of the bikers she found on the road periodically did, she still didn't fully trust him. His nickname, Tapper, closed several possibilities for her, one being opening her heart to him. There was no way she'd allow herself to become vulnerable in front of a womanizer. A man who only sought to conquer the precious treasure between a woman's thighs and then leave. She learned harsh lessons from the past idiots she dated. She thought she'd never fall for a suave, charismatic male again. She was wrong.

Tania happily sighed as Weldon drove through a heavily wooded area. The crisp smell of autumn teased her nostrils while they zipped through small piles of red-orange-colored leaves, flitting about on the side of the road. She loved this time of year. She'd enjoy sharing it with someone worthy to stand by her side. She once thought her fiancée was that special someone. —Her stomach cringed in response to the sudden onslaught of emotions washing through her. Why couldn't she easily pick out the good guys and leave the undesirables behind? Yet, she gave everyone the benefit of the doubt, and that was her problem.

Weldon pulled under a tall, leafy tree and switched off the bike. He helped her off the machine and then dismounted, assisting her with removing her helmet and securing it to the back of his bike. She glanced around her, marveling at the gorgeous colors surrounding them when he said her name. Turning toward him, she found his outstretched hand, waiting for her to take it. She stared at his open palm for several long seconds, contemplating what to do. They weren't a couple, and touching him anymore placed her in jeopardy of losing her keen willpower. Placing her small hand in his, she reminded herself to remain strong as he escorted her to one of several picnic benches nearby.

He lifted a leg over the bench and sat sideways, looking at her as she mimicked his posture and took a seat in front of him. Bending her right leg toward her, she rested it atop the wooden slats. She leaned her upper body toward the long, rectangular table in front of her, resting her weight on her right elbow.

Weldon started. "So, are you going to tell me why you've been avoiding me? I thought we had a good time."

She snorted. "You don't mince words, do you?"

"You haven't returned any of my calls. I just want to know where we stand."

"We? Weldon, there's no we."

"There could be."

She uttered a noise in disagreement. Her eyebrows furrowed together. "Do you know your nickname at the bar I work at?"

"You mean Tapper?"

Her mouth formed an "O ." "If you know, then why are you asking me why I didn't call?"

He leaned toward her and looked into her eyes. "Do you also know that I always leave the girl I'm with at daybreak? But this time, I didn't have the chance."

Tania gasped. "Is that how you feel about me? I'm just another notch in your belt?" He grabbed her arm as she shot off the bench. Gently, he pulled her back down. "Why am I here, Weldon? Why did you bring me here if you're only going to insult me? I want to leave."

"You didn't give me a chance to finish. I normally take off and leave my bedmates behind. I don't pursue any of them unless I want another fling-"

She screeched and bucked out of her seat to try to stand. Weldon bolted toward her. He threw his arms around her, containing her within a tight embrace.

She squirmed, attempting to release his arms. "No, please. Leave me alone. I don't want to be another one of your conquests."

His warm breath caressed her neck and sent shivers down her spine. She rolled her eyes back with the pleasant sensation. "I don't want that, either."

She glanced up at him. "What? What are you saying? You just told me you didn't have a chance to leave me. I left you, instead."

"Yes."

She stared into his beautiful irises, now bright green, which lulled her into a false sense of security. She picked at words in her brain to form a semi-adequate response.

"I don't know what you want."

"I want a chance with you."

She laughed. "You can't be serious. You're the Tapper. Weldon, I don't trust you." She wriggled out of his embrace.

"You don't know me."

"That's true, but I know enough about you to know better than to trust you."

He chuckled and lifted his hands into the air in a show of surrender. "Fair enough. I guess you've already pre-judged me based on my past, and I can't convince you otherwise. I will just have to show you, then."

She pointed toward the road. "You think you can do that? There are so many temptations out there."

He beckoned toward her. "There's one right in front of me."

She widened her eyes. "I don't know what to make of you."

"Give me a chance."

She picked at a stained spot on the bench. "A tiger doesn't change its stripes."

"Yes, but a wolf mates for life."

She shook her head. "What? You're confusing me. What does one have to do with the other?"

"I'm just stating a fact."

"Are you comparing yourself to a wolf and me, to your mate?"

The corners of his mouth curled up into a smile.

"We only had one night."

"We can remedy that, I'm sure," Weldon said.

She pushed off the bench and stood next to him, her hands crossed in front of her chest. "I-I don't know what to say. This whole conversation has gone off course, somehow, and has become very strange."

"Besides the idea that you have in your head that I bed hop, tell me what made you leave my house so quickly and before I got up?" She stared at him but didn't answer his question. How could she tell him she was scared he might be the one for her?

He brushed his hand across hers. "Tania, tell me the truth. How do you feel about me?"

She bit her lower lip, contemplating what to do. There was no way she could tell him how she felt about him. He'd take advantage of her or, worse, play with her until he grew tired of her, breaking her heart in the process when he finally left her for good. Focusing her attention on the road, she calculated if she could run, or more likely, jog to freedom. How far away were they from civilization? Was there a house close by where she could call an Uber? That's if the company even served this area. Weldon tapped his fingers across the table. In his red bandana and leather jacket, he was gorgeous. His skin-tight leather pants did nothing to settle her frazzled nerves. He always seemed to wear clothing one to two sizes smaller, or maybe he only did so when he visited her. Still, there was no denying the man was smoking hot, and he knew it. Maybe she should have one more night with him as a final goodbye. This time, she'd enjoy every minute of his body next to hers. Every single second of the firm ripped, muscular physique, she wanted, desperately, to run her tongue all over.

He leaned over his elbows and looked straight at her. "I'm waiting —"

Weldon demanded an answer. She didn't want to give one. What in the hell was she going to do now?

Chapter Eight

Tania's gaze brushed over the grass by his boots.

"You feel something for me. I know you do. That's why you don't want to answer me."

Damn. The man was on point.

Her gaze swept the forest once more. She wondered if she could outrun him. Yet, she'd never been a marathon runner. Quite the opposite. She always ended up last in any race.

His fingers caressing the side of her cheek sent sexy shivers straight through her. It was as if he knew the effect he had on her. He was tempting her, inviting her to feast on his impeccable body. To indulge in every fantasy, she envisioned. She swallowed hard, allowing her gaze to capture every last bit of him from head to toe. She needed to satisfy the intense craving building up within her, urging her to enjoy one last, fantastical night with the man, but her subconscious, ultimately, wanted her to be the one for him. She couldn't cover up reality with fantasy. Weldon wasn't boyfriend material.

He was a one-time thrill and a salacious dream she never thought possible.

"I know you feel something for me. Whether you like it or not, you're drawn to me as I am to you. I want you, Tania."

Tania ran. Her heartbeat kicked up as she strove to add miles between them. She had no idea where she was going or where she'd end up but getting far away from Weldon was her only goal at the moment. The more she ran, the more distance she placed between them, and the easier she felt. What Weldon said to her was comical. Of course,, he wanted her. She was a female, alone, in the woods with him.

Stupid. That's what she was. She let him drive her here only to leave her vulnerable in an unknown park, forest, or wherever she was. Now, she had no transportation back.

She scurried around a tree and braced her arms in front of her when she tipped forward. There was no way she was falling to the ground like those helpless females in horror movies she'd watched in the past. Whatever happened, she had to remain swift but careful. She looped around another tree, crying out when the bark sliced part of her finger. Shoving the hand in front of her, she glanced as droplets of blood slid from the cut. It was as if she were witnessing an artist painting a portrait. She swiped the finger across her clothing, not caring if the color mismatched the ones on her ensemble. When she heard an extra set of footsteps behind her, she attempted to run faster, but her little legs were already at maximum speed.

Her heart skipped a beat when she heard a low rumbling sound. Damn. Was there wildlife in the forest, too? She should've brought her mace or, better yet, a Taser. With their sudden departure, she brought nothing but her purse, currently slung over her shoulder. Maybe she should toss the bag at the animal running after her. Would that slow it down? Of course, she'd have to aim for its nose- a feat that would mean she'd have to stop and take the time to aim at the animal as if it had a target on its head. She doubted she'd have the time or the skill to sling the purse at the wild beast before it ate her for lunch.

The beast leaped at her as her traitorous legs slowed down. Damn her out-of-shape body. If only she had used that annual pass to the gym, she purchased at a substantial discount, online. Yet, in her free time, the last thing she wanted to do was test or challenge it with perspiration and breathlessness. Her body slammed the dirt floor underneath the thing that trapped her. With its warm breath pressed to her ear, she yelped when the creature growled. Her heartbeat skipped several beats while she took long seconds to figure out what to do. Should she stay put and hope it disappeared versus slashing her to death? Or should she claw at it and run? That's if she was able to get back onto her feet without it taking her down.

Her eyes widened when hands, not paws, turned her around to face him. Weldon stared straight into her eyes.

"Do I scare you? Why did you run?"

Did he trade places with the mythical creature? She could've sworn the thing pounded after her through the forest, chasing her into the unfortunate predicament she found herself in. Under normal circumstances, she wouldn't complain about being this close to a gorgeous man panting for breath. Especially with a look in his eye that told her she could be his next meal if he ended up a predator. Finding some kind of ink under his shirt, she shoved at it and stared at the profile of some animal. Maybe he was the beast, after all. Yeah. If she believed in fairy tales or paranormal romance stories.

She traced the lines of the solid black figure, marveling at its beauty. "What's this?"

"It's a wolf."

"Oh? You like them?"

His wide grin displayed perfect white teeth. "Yeah. I like them a lot. Do you?"

She looked up at him and smiled. "Yes. They're beautiful animals."

"You can touch me if you want."

She wanted to, desperately, but the fact that he bedded women faster than she blinked her eyes set her on edge.

"Oh —you don't know how I want to —" Did she just say that out loud? Her eyes widened with her confession. The corners of his mouth curled up into a salacious grin.

"Indulge in your fantasies with me, Tania."

She closed her eyes and shook her head. "No. I can't. You're bad for me."

"How do you know? Listening to all the rumors instead of what's in your heart?" Without warning, he grabbed her index finger and sucked on it. Of all things that were holy! Squirrely sensations shot through her, strumming straight to her girly parts and leaving her stunned and wanting more. He kept up the sucking motion, eying her while she moaned and writhed on the ground. Images of doing the same to a certain amazing appendage between his legs grabbed at her. It urged her to yank the finger from between his teeth and tear his pants off to fulfill the fantasy. Then they, both, would end up satisfied. With one last hard suck, he held the finger up, triumphant as he slid something from between his teeth.

He licked his lips, cleansing them of every drop of her blood. Closing his eyes, he breathed in slowly and groaned. "Splinter." He held the transparent object up and then flung it into a nearby bush before he brought her finger to his lips and took one last, long lick. Holy crap. She had to be in hell, for what he did to her was pure torture.

"You taste so good." The strange words from his lips didn't register in her brain. Instead, she focused on getting away.

"Please—" She thought the single word she spoke, and the pleading look in her eyes would shake him enough to let her go. She was wrong.

His eye color darkened, and an unquenched hunger passed across his face. "That's what I like to hear."

Suddenly, he smothered her with his manly musk and his powerful arms, teasing and tormenting her with overwhelming pleasure until she submitted to his sexy demands. She glanced down and found her bottom half-naked. How in the devil did that happen?

With one single swoop, Weldon stripped off his pants and underwear. Tania gasped as her gaze swept over him. The awakened leviathan below bounced and grew with her ardent attention. My lord. Weldon was amazing. She was too drunk the first time to truly notice all that he possessed.

He grinned as he repositioned himself over her. She sighed, her eyes rolling to the back of her head as she felt him at her entrance.

"You are so wet," he whispered. He kissed across her cheek, caressing the side of his face against hers in an almost loving manner. The beard stubble grazing lightly over her soft skin forced a giggle from her mouth.

He ran his thumb across her parted lips and gave her a sweet smile. "You are truly gorgeous."

How many women had he shared the same sentiment with before?

"Are you ready?"

She widened her eyes and gulped back the indecision screaming at her brain, attempting to stop her from making another mistake. A hidden, weaker part of her wanted him. She wasn't passing up the opportunity to enjoy him this time. She dug her heels into his bare bottom. He lowered his mouth and graced hers with a kiss. At the same time, he pushed forward. She uttered a sound, barely audible beneath his rough grunt. Shoving her hands through strands of his hair, she tugged while he took her on the most magnificent journey of her life. He was aggressive, assertive, and demanding. She succumbed like prey caught by a predator. Like a comfortable, snug blanket wrapped around her, all she saw, felt, and sensed was Weldon. It was wonderful. Sadly, the time spent with him passed too quickly.

SHE OPENED HER EYES and squinted at him through the darkness. Lord. Did she just. —Once with him was, apparently, not enough for her, so she gave him, her body, twice. And damn, she had the best sex of her life, again, with. —a cad and a womanizer. Shit. What in the hell was she thinking? That he'd turn over a new leaf for her? She wanted to laugh, but her heart was already broken by the idea no woman would ever claim him, least of all, her. She was a struggling bartender, after all. She had nothing to offer the gorgeous playboy.

She shoved off the leather jacket he placed beneath her knees when he took her from behind. She quivered. A delightful thrill rippled through her insides as she recalled the experience. The sex was rough like he was trying to brand her or something. Still, she loved his possessiveness and the way he held her gently while he took control. More than anything, she wanted to awaken from the fantasy world she created for the two of them and find out that it was all real.

If only he cared about her. If only he'd remain loyal.

The wolf tattoo on his upper chest and the sexual position he preferred both indicated a sexy, feral nature. Yet, when he made the growling noises. —He only made the unusual noise a few times during their tryst. Never before experiencing a lover making unusual sounds during sex, the noise he made shocked her at first... After a while, though, she looked forward to them as they reminded her that he wanted her- a concept she still couldn't quite grasp. Was she another notch on his bedpost, or was he seeking something different with her? Weldon wasn't like her past boyfriends. He, definitely, was nothing like her current bedmates. He was, somehow, different. Intriguing. A mystery she'd love to reveal in full, one day. If he stayed loyal.

She unstuck herself from his sinfully gorgeous chest and whined when he grabbed at her arm and pulled her back to him.

"Where are you going, sexy?"

She wondered if he called all his bedmates that term. "I have to go."

He placed his arms behind his head and gazed at her. "You don't work tonight."

"Oh? You know my schedule now?" She handed him the red bandana she pulled off his head during their first sexual encounter of the night. The red color was a perfect match for his rebellious personality and his love for personal freedom.

He waved a hand at her. "You keep it. It will look better on you, anyway."

She tilted her head to one side. "Souvenir?"

"Gift. From me to you."

A gift? That's what the incredible experience of having sex with him was. This was a second gift: a reminder of his warm body and his musky scent as he held her within his strong, powerful arms. It was also proof that she'd enjoyed the "Tapper" as so many others had in his past.

She rolled the fabric between her fingers before she strapped the bandana above her elbow.

He pointed to her arm. "Looks good on you."

It did, actually. Part of her wanted to shed tears in mourning for what would never be. At least she had a reminder of the good times.

"Take me home."

She strolled to the bike and grabbed the helmet off the back of it when she remembered she cut her finger, earlier, on tree bark. Bringing the index finger closer, she eyeballed it but couldn't find the area that bled only several hours ago. Where did the cut go?

Weldon grabbed the helmet from her hands and lifted it over her head, placing it gently on her. "I healed you."

Her mouth agape, she glanced up at him. "Huh? Seriously?"

"Yeah. Something in my saliva does that." He winked. "Yeah, I know. I'm unusual."

She stared at him as he straddled the bike.

"You going to get on, or do I need to come to get you like I did when you tried to run from me?"

She tried to move, but she couldn't get over the fact that he healed people with his saliva. What was he?

"Have you always been able to do that? Heal people."

"Yeah. Just minor things. It's not like I can lick your whole body and heal it, though I'd be willing to try." He gave her another wink paired with a salacious grin.

Oh lord! The scandalous images flooding her brain had her ready to lie back down in the grass and let him experiment with her. Yet, nothing changed. He remained wrong for her.

He eased off the bike and strolled toward her before she had the chance to issue a verbal warning. Running his hands up and down her forearms, he whispered,

"Do you really want to go back home? Let's go to my place, instead."

Pleasant vibes shot straight through her. Lord! Was she always going to end up in his bed? His proposition was too tempting. She had to remain strong.

She shook her head. "No. I have to go home. Kara is probably worried about me."

He gave her a wry smile. "Sure. Okay. I'll take you home."

She followed him to the bike, a tinge of regret stabbing through the deepest recesses of her fragile heart.

TANIA EXHALED A SIGH of relief as she realized one entire week passed with no sign of Weldon. Granted, he left her several voicemails after their impromptu reunion in the woods. When she didn't return his phone calls, he left her one final message two days ago stating he was making a run for his company. He said he'd be back next week. She wasn't holding her breath.

The urge to erase his number from her contacts gnawed at her. Still, she couldn't do it. If she did, she wouldn't be able to easily avoid his calls. As fun as spending time with Weldon proved to be, she didn't trust herself around him. As proof, she only had to recall what happened in the forest a week ago. Lord, it was fun, yet she couldn't give in to a pipe dream. There were several qualities she wanted in a boyfriend, traits she wasn't going to renege on. One of them was loyalty. With the nickname '*Tapper*,' he already failed.

Instead of dwelling on the relationship she'd never hope to have with the handsome rebel, she went back to her old life. She started seeing some of her regulars again. There were only a few casual friends she bounced between when she *needed* a man. Sometimes sex toys didn't satisfy the need. A warm, live body was what one desired during those occasions.

Yet, she didn't choose just anyone to warm her bed. *Hell no.* After the louses she hooked up with in the past, trusting someone came slowly to her. That's why there were only three lucky souls that had her number and her company when fun was offered.

The fact that Weldon happened in between her regulars was —well —unexplainable. There was something about him she liked. Maybe it was the sexy smirk he gave her at times. Maybe it was the swagger of his hips or the honest-sounding words pouring out of his mouth. Whatever it was, she fell for him and hard. Now, she was trying to retreat before he came back for her. If he walked into the bar right now, she might have to leap over the damn counter and make a break for it be-

fore he sat down. Spending just two seconds in his company
with his musky male scent entwining with his sexy, gruff voice
would be the end for her. Falling to the floor behind the bar,
she'd open her thighs and invite him in before he could say another word.

Yeah. She had it bad. She knew it now. That's why she
didn't trust herself around him.

There was something about Weldon that lied to her. Made
her think things might be different with him. Until she recalled
his nickname.

"Here you go," she said, greeting a new customer and placing the drink she ordered in front of her. "If you need anything
else, let me know."

The customer slid the drink closer. "You're friends with
Weldon."

Tania stared at her. Speechless at first, her throat worked,
but she had trouble forming any intelligible words. "I wouldn't
call him a friend, but I do know him. Why do you want to
know?"

The dark-haired woman twirled the two thin black straws.
Her gaze focused on the liquid swirling within the clear glass.
"He's an asshole."

That piqued her curiosity. She chuckled. "You must know
him, then."

The stranger held her hand out in front of her. Tania shook
it in response. "I'm Eva, by the way."

"Tania. You're new here?"

"Yeah, I had to check out the place Weldon likes coming to.
Now, I know why." She winked. "Don't worry, I'm not check-

ing up on you, for him, though I will warn you, he likes you. But like I said, he's an asshole. At least I thought so, at first."

"How do you know him?"

"I'm married to his brother."

Tania slapped a hand over her mouth. "Oh. I'm sorry. I didn't mean—"

"It's okay. Weldon and I aren't friends. Not really. We tolerate each other. He's nothing like his brother, as you can imagine. I wouldn't have married him if he was." She laughed.

Tania leaned over the counter. "So, why are you here?"

Eva raised her glass in a toast before she lowered it to her lips. "I wanted to get to know you and have a good drink. Plus, if you want to know anything about him, I'm an open book. I won't mince words or paint a pretty picture of him. He's a cad, but I will say he has a good heart, too. He means well. He just doesn't know how to express it. Like I said, he and his brother, Kingsley, are very different. Where Kingsley is sensitive, caring, and endearing, Weldon's a dick. He's insensitive, unrelenting, and loves his freedom. He's not tied down to anyone or anything, and that's how he likes it. Yet, he can't stop talking about you. There's something about you he really likes. The way he talks about you is different. He respects you."

Tania's eyebrows furrowed. "He does?" Eva nodded. A list of questions whirled around in Tania's brain. She wanted to know everything. Yet overwhelming poor Eva with her curiosity wasn't her intention. "So, can I ask how you came to know his brother and then him?"

Eva dropped her empty glass to the counter and smiled. "Well. How much time do you have?"

Tania picked up the bottle to her left and tipped its contents into Eva's glass. She stopped when the amber liquid settled just underneath the etched horizontal line she used as a makeshift measuring device. "I get off in four hours."

Eva lifted the glass to her lips. "Good. We have plenty of time."

Chapter Nine

Weldon parked the truck in his secret spot behind Kingsley's cabin. With only a condo to his name, he had no way of stashing the truck anywhere. Yet, Kingsley, learning of his brother's plight, loaned the empty area behind the cabin for his use and poured cement onto the dirt so that Weldon could park his truck there at any time. If it wasn't for his brother, he'd have to pay for a garage to stash the vehicle. Yet, Kingsley applauded Weldon's entrepreneurial spirit and his lofty goal of earning extra income on his own terms. After all, Kingsley was a businessman himself, owning a comfortable, successful establishment called the White Wolf Inn for more than a decade.

Affixing the red bandana on his head, which he purchased recently from a store, he pulled leather gloves over his hands, grabbed his helmet, and stalked over to his bike. When he spotted movement from the corner of his eye, he whipped toward it and growled, one fang extended over his bottom lip.

A robed figure held one hand out in front of her as she rose to a stand. "It's just me."

"Eva? What are you doing out this late? Is Kingsley with you?" Weldon glanced back at the cabin.

"He's asleep. Typical. He gets to slumber peacefully while I take on all our worries." She sighed. "I decided to do something constructive, instead. That's why I'm out here."

He glanced down at the rose petals, a translucent glass bowl that held some kind of fragrant liquid, and several white candles that must've been lit at one point and guessed at the conclusion. Eva had been casting a spell. It was either that or something else along those lines. Weldon didn't understand what Wicca was. Only that she believed in it and following the religion did no harm. That was enough.

She pushed her hood back from her head and shook her hair out from beneath it. "Have some time to sit with me?"

Weldon glanced, longingly, at his bike before his gaze boomeranged back to her. She never offered to speak with him, alone, before. If she was asking him now, there had to be a reason. She was his sister-in-law, after all. He couldn't let her down. "Sure."

He followed her up to the porch. One snap of her fingers sent electricity coursing through the light bulb overhead and forced an open-mouthed gasp from Weldon.

"I'll never get used to that," he confessed.

"It was once a curse. It's a gift, now. Sit." She pointed to the rocking chair closest to him.

He placed the helmet on the table between them before he lowered himself into the wooden seat. His legs instantly started a slow rocking motion that soothed the growing tension zipping through his veins. What did she want to talk to him about? Were she and Kingsley having problems? If so, he was the last person in the world she should come to for romantic advice.

"I met Tania today."

His heart stopped, along with the motion of his chair. "What did you say?"

"I said I met Tania. She's a sweet girl. Lovely too. What in the hell do you want with her?"

A rolling growl escaped Weldon's lips. "She's my mate."

"I think you're getting the better end of the deal here."

Weldon braced his hands on the arms of the rocker and bolted to a stand. He leaned over Eva and snarled. Unaffected by his action, Eva continued rocking. "Do you want to hear what happened or do you want to continue your possessive streak?"

He made a half-snorting sound, took several steps back, and sat down. During the long moment of frustrating silence, he waited to capture every word regarding Eva's experience with the captivating bombshell he wanted desperately bonded to him. The problem was that Tania wouldn't give him the time of day, much less offer him the grand opportunity for another sinful go with her delectable body.

"I see why you like her. In the few hours we spent together talking, I find her funny, smart, and genuine. Definitely not who I thought you'd end up with." Eva chuckled. "She likes you, you know. She confessed it to me."

Weldon's head popped up. "She did? She hasn't returned any of my calls."

"She's scared. She doesn't trust you, either. Wait till she finds out what you truly are. That is unless you've told her?"

He shook his head.

"She's seeing a few men." His pained whine interrupted her. "Nothing serious, though. You don't have to worry. But if I were you, I'd pounce on the fact that she likes you. Something draws her to you, but she'd never confessed it. I saw how much she likes you by the way her eyes lit up each time I said your name. I also sensed her attraction to you."

His heartbeats picked up speed, galloping with the thrilling sensation whirling about his heart. "Really? That's all I've ever wanted to hear. That she feels the same way about me as I do her."

Eva nodded. "She does. But you need to break down those barriers that are separating her from you. It won't be easy, gaining her trust, but it'll be worth it. She's a good woman. One I'd love to welcome into our family."

Weldon's grin mimicked Eva's smile. "I didn't know you were going to see her."

"I was curious. Besides, I have a responsibility to find out who might become a permanent part of our tribe and make sure she's good enough for you."

He snorted. "I didn't think you liked me."

"Of course, I do, Weldon. You're Kingsley's brother. And even though we didn't hit it off well when we first met, I've come to know you since then. You're not all bad."

"Neither are you. I see why my brother married you."

Eva giggled. "That and my good looks and smoking hot bod."

As if on cue, Kingsley stepped onto the porch. "What's going on out here?" His hand on his hips, he glanced between them with half-lidded eyes. "Weldon, is everything okay?"

Weldon glanced over at Eva and nodded his thanks. "It is now." He grabbed his helmet and lifted from the rocking chair. "I have to go. See you two later." They watched Weldon as he stepped off the porch and made his way over to his bike.

With sudden cat-like reflexes, Kingsley slipped over to Eva's side. She stood for mere seconds before he scooped her into his arms. "I don't know what you and Weldon were talking about, but at this moment, I don't care. I want you in our bed right now. If you couldn't sleep, you should've woken me up. I would've taken care of you as I'm going to now." He stalked through the door and slammed it behind him. Eva's giggles were soon muffled by Kingsley's lips.

"WHY WON'T YOU GO OUT with me?"

Weldon's words jolted Tania out of her mental fog. She had to say something. Weldon wouldn't give up. Still, the idea of him walking away from her pierced a fragile part of her heart she didn't know existed. The thought of never seeing him or talking to him again tore through her insides. She wanted something with Weldon though she wasn't sure what. Since he couldn't be trusted, a long-term relationship was out of the question. Tania would never be satisfied as friends, and the idea of friends with benefits swirled a spiky, painful sadness through her stomach. For the first time in a long time, Tania didn't know what to do. How did she let him down when she didn't give him an opportunity?

She shook her head. "I can't. I know you don't understand."

Weldon slapped down several bills onto the countertop and lifted off the barstool. "Yet you have no trouble going out with other men."

Something within her protested when he turned to leave. Before she knew what she was doing, her hand shot out in an attempt to stop him. "Wait!" Several patrons at the bar turned toward her. She drew in a deep breath and collected her thoughts before she did anything that would warrant further attention. She was on the clock, after all.

Sweeping past the edge of the countertop, she called out to her counterpart on the restaurant floor and told him she'd be on break. Next, she headed toward Weldon, catching his eyebrows furrowing together when she grabbed ahold of his arm. Leading Weldon toward the exit of the door, she glanced back at her counterpart and found a smirk settling across his face. She didn't care what he or any of the others at the establishment thought about Weldon. They could come up with all the nicknames in the world for him, and it wouldn't matter. All the stories they conjured up, whether real or not, didn't take away the fascination she had for him.

She swiveled toward the narrow alleyway between the buildings outside the door and then stopped to face Weldon. She placed her hands on her hips. "Why are you interested in me, anyway? You've already had sex with me several times. Aren't you supposed to tap me and then move on?"

He sniggered. "Do you know how cute you are when you're upset?"

"Oh please. —Don't patronize me."

"I'm serious. If you don't know by now that I like you, Tania, I don't know what I need to do to convince you. I don't want to tap you. I want to date you."

Her throat, suddenly, went dry. She coughed, placing her hand around her throat when the cough turned into hacking. His amused look quickly switched to concern.

He placed a hand on her shoulder as she doubled over with fits. "Are you okay? Should I get you a glass of water?"

Lifting up, she shook her head. She placed her hand out in front of her, gesturing to him to give her a minute. Placing her hand across her forehead, she rubbed it for a few seconds before she sighed. "I don't know what you want from me."

"I want to date you."

She muttered under her breath. "No."

"Why not? Am I not worth a chance?"

Weldon would break her heart. How did she tell him that without hurting his feelings? According to Eva, Weldon liked variety. He craved adventure. He liked fun. He wasn't one to settle down. Tania preferred the same, but now that she met Weldon, her ideas regarding what she did and didn't want no longer made sense. She pictured a future with the sexy as hell rogue standing in front of her. Still, she wasn't willing to sacrifice her heart when what she envisioned didn't work out. Breakups were hell.

"It's okay. I understand."

"I'm sorry, Weldon. I like you. I really do but —"

"I understand. You can't get over the Tapper nickname. I get it. I regret my past now."

Damn. She felt low. Her heart missed a beat when she caught Weldon's marked frown. He was sad, and it was all because of her. God, she was horrible.

She pulled him to her and kissed him. He resisted, at first, placing his hands on her shoulders to stop her. Then, he gave in to their slow, sweet kiss. His shoulders relaxed. The tension in his arms dissipated. He pulled her into him and deepened the kiss, causing a moan to escape through her lips.

He looked into her eyes as he hovered over her. "Damn it, Tania. I wish you'd give me a chance. We'd be good together."

Hell. He might be right. Still, she couldn't risk her heart for the false promise of a remarkably vivid dream.

Weldon tightened his arms around her waist and drew her in for another passionate kiss.

"I want you, Tania. Let me take you somewhere. Let's have fun and then head back to my place."

"I can't, Weldon. I have to head back."

"Later, then. I'll come by and pick you up."

God, how she wanted to say yes. She slipped out of his arms and straightened her clothes. Giving him one last, longing glance, she swept her index finger across the beard stubble lingering on his cheek. "I have to go." She swiveled away and headed back to the restaurant.

She swallowed the dry lump forming in the back of her throat while attempting to quell the aching emptiness in her heart. No matter what she did, she'd never fulfill whatever Weldon sought from her. As she turned the corner, she sensed him still watching her. If only Weldon was a different man. If only he wasn't Weldon.

WELDON DIDN'T KNOW what to do to convince the curvaceous bombshell of his true intentions. Unlike women in his past, he wasn't attempting to make Tania another notch on his bedpost. If he wanted that, he would've left her shortly after their erotic play in the park. The delicious morsel already gave it up to him an incredible four times. Weldon came back for her the other night after their steamy encounter in the alley outside her workplace. He didn't give her a chance to protest. Instead, he immediately fanned the flames of her passion with deep kisses and purposeful touches that spiked her libido and his, as well. Learning of her love for Mexican food, he took her to a favorite of his- a Taco food truck only a few miles from the bar. Then he brought her home for dessert.

Four times of the most amazing sex he ever had, and the woman still didn't want to have anything to do with him. It was impossible. As a hybrid, she should've been immediate, drawn to his magnetism, incapable of saying "no." That's how it was with most women he encountered. If his wolf didn't have females opening their thighs for him, his vampire did. Yet, Tania proved the exception. Although she, eventually, gave in to his charm nearly every time their encounters grew heated, she still *wanted* to say no. That frustrated Weldon. There had to be a way to encourage her to say yes, permanently.

Yet, when his phone chimed her familiar set tone, he stared at the screen blank-faced with confusion whirling about in his head. He pressed the green button before she had a chance to change her mind.

"Hello?" He said into the receiver, awaiting her response. He got dead air instead. He, faintly, heard her voice in the background and a familiar metallic, clicking noise that, sporadically, turned on and off. Then he heard her frustrated groan, followed by a few expletives.

"Start, damn you, start." She pounded something hard and sighed loudly. It sounded like she needed help.

He ended the call, quickly pressed a series of buttons on his screen, and located her phone. After one of their *engagements*, he programmed the secretive device into her phone without her notice. He imagined what she'd say to him if she knew he was able to track her, anywhere. He grinned as her pouty lips formed another round of expletives meant just for him. He didn't care what she thought. As his mate, his mission was to keep her safe at all times. If that meant implanting an app into her phone or a GPS system into her body while she remained unaware, so be it. As long as it caused her no physical pain, he was all for it.

He recalled the bruises he received after Kingsley found out he planted the device on Eva's phone. Weldon expressed mild surprise, not finding the device on the phone already. Apparently, Kingsley trusted her or was attempting to trust her. Not Weldon. He didn't know Eva. If she tried anything with Kingsley, he wanted the ability to find his brother and stop her before she caused any further harm. Yet when Kingsley found the device, he knew exactly who planted it on her phone. That ended up in a beating Weldon didn't care to remember. Both of them suffered bruises and split lips that night.

Grabbing his keys, he headed out the door and aimed his car in the direction of a local retail store parking lot in the next county. He accelerated the Vette to speeds just over the posted speed limit but still within a safe cushion of responsibility. Whether she owned up to it or not, his mate needed him, and he wasn't going to let her down. If his car could fly, he'd be there already. Still, he aimed to help her out in any way he could. Even if that meant taking her home in the hot rod he only used on special occasions.

He swooped into the parking lot and canvassed the area when he spotted her car. As luck would have it, he found an empty parking space directly across from her. The odds of that occurring humbled his temporary glee. The stars seemed aligned, tonight, for them. If only —

Alighting from his car, he stalked over to her side to find her not in the car. Where did she go? He scanned the parking lot and the front of the building. Not finding her, he lifted his phone and dialed her number, placing the phone to his ear when it went straight to voicemail.

"Tanis, this is Weldon. I'm here in your car. I know you need help. Please come back to your car." Punching the red button, he ended the call and slid his phone down the back pocket of his jeans. He waited for several minutes. Leaning his rear against the fender, he warded off female interest by keeping his head down or looking away as their eyes spotted him across the parking lot. Damn. Where was she?

Since she came into his life, he had little interest in the opposite sex. With the nickname Tapper, it was laughable that he would shy away from what he used to enjoy. Yet, the fact remained, if he couldn't have Tania, he didn't want anyone. He wasn't searching anymore.

Not that he sought a permanent union with anyone. He had no interest in solidifying anything with anyone, that is until Tania walked into the picture. Now, images of her flooded his head throughout his days. He wanted her. He needed to make things permanent with her. She was the one meant for him. Second, best wasn't good enough. Besides, she had that sultry, unique scent he couldn't get enough of, and her blood type was the right match for his hungry other half. He'd suck on the grade A liquid a little each day to feed his desire for her if she let him. The act of biting into her delicate skin threatened his fangs to grow. She, too, would enjoy the pull of his lips on her tasty essence. He knew this because drunken females in his past with no idea how they received the bite marks welcomed the orgasmic rush as he feasted on their liquid gift.

Of course, Tania wasn't like the others. She never would be. She was unduplicated. If she only accepted him... He slipped his phone out of his back pocket and glanced down at the screen, willing her name to appear. Damn, the woman was stubborn. How did he break down her walls when she wouldn't let him near her?

He tried her number again, promptly ending the call when he spotted her walking out a side door with a man beside her. He slid his phone back into his pocket and waited for her to approach. The start of a smile curled up the corners of his mouth when he caught her surprised look.

"What are you doing here?"

"I heard you were having car problems."

She stared up at him with an incredulous look across her face amidst the stark silence. "How did you—"

An unfamiliar voice interrupted them. "I guess you don't need my help then. I'll head back inside if you're good here." The man thumbed at the large building behind him.

Her hand shot out in a stopping motion to the stranger. "Um, wait a minute. I don't know if Weldon has a car or even owns one. I need a jump."

Weldon grinned. "You must not have remembered." He pointed toward the canary-colored Corvette opposite of her car.

Her jaw dropped. "You own that?" He nodded. "But aren't you not supposed to jump cars with that thing?"

Weldon fired back. "That thing can take care of your car just fine." He motioned toward the stranger. "Thank you for your help. We won't be needing it after all. I'm here now."

Tania glanced over her shoulder at the stranger as he walked away. "Uh, thanks, anyway. I appreciate it." She turned back toward Weldon. "Are you sure? I wouldn't want you to hurt your investment. I'm sure you spent a precious bundle on that one.

He smirked. "What do you have against Corvettes? You need help, right? I'll deal with the consequences later if there are any." He lifted the trunk up and brought out the jumper cables. "Now, pop open the hood." She did as he instructed, and he went to work attaching the cables to their respective battery terminals.

"I don't have anything against Corvettes. They're just flashy cars. They're also extremely uncomfortable to get into. My dad used to own one. I hated it."

Weldon laughed. "I'll keep that in mind when I decide to purchase another automobile. In the meantime, why don't you get into my car and press the start button on it?"

She pointed to herself. "Me? You want me to get into your car?"

"Sure. I have to make sure everything is okay on this end. I need someone to start the car and eventually rev the engine. You see anyone else around?"

She mumbled under her breath as she strolled toward his car. "Don't be such a smartass."

He laughed. "That's my middle name, sweetheart."

Chapter Ten

Weldon watched with amusement in his eyes as Tania contorted and wriggled her body, struggling to get into his car. Eventually, she dropped into the driver's seat with a "whoomph" and semi-cursed at the machine as she shimmied her bottom against the leather seat to try to reach the gas pedal. Damn. She was cute. Tawdry images popped into his head. What he wouldn't do to take her over his knee right now and give her a valuable lesson in respecting other people's property.

He tried formulating a plan to stick around after her car started, that's if it did. When the car finally sputtered alive, she rejoiced while he removed the cables and slammed the hoods down. Then he made his way to her open window.

"So, where to now?" His heart remained hopeful that she wouldn't shove him away- not after a gallant rescue effort.

"Thank you, Weldon, for helping me. How did you know I was here?"

He pointed toward her cellphone poking out from her purse. "Your phone. You butt-dialed me."

She clapped her hands over her mouth. "Oh! That's funny. I was thinking about calling you, but I didn't. It must've dialed the last number I had on the screen."

"Why didn't you call me? I would've come by and helped you."

"I didn't want to bother you, and Kara was busy. I had no one else I could turn to."

He leaned over the windowsill. "You can always count on me. If I'm in the area, I will gladly help."

She bit her lower lip but didn't reply.

"I wish you'd trust me." His shoulders dropped, followed by a long sigh. "You have groceries in your backseat. I better let you go."

"Why don't you come with me?"

His frown turned into a hopeful grin. "Where are you going?"

"To the apartment, but if you'll follow me and you're okay with it, I'd like to drop my car off at the shop first and then go home. Is that okay?"

He nodded. "Of course. But won't Kara be at the apartment?"

"Yeah. I'm cooking for her tonight. You don't have to worry about her. She's moved on. She has a boyfriend now."

"Really? That's good to hear. She won't mind if I tag along?"

She giggled. "Weldon. You rescued me. You're good. Besides, I think I owe you a meal, too." Tania glanced back at his car. "Is it okay if I put my groceries in your car, though? Some of the bags might be wet from condensation."

He flipped his keys in the air and winked. "It's fine. That's what I have a trunk for. I'll follow you." As he climbed into the driver's seat of his car, he realized how true that statement was. He'd gladly follow her, anywhere she went, as long as she belonged to him and no one else. This last little tidbit regarding loyalty and fidelity he'd have to impress upon her once she was ready to accept him. Until then, he'd emulate the example he expected from her. It was Tania or no one.

SINCE HIS CHIVALROUS act at the retail store, Tania let Weldon in —a little. The fact that she was, somehow, crazily drawn to him did nothing to stop or sort out the ping-ponging back and forth wave of her emotions. Should she date him or not? They remained friends who spent time in each other's company and sometimes in each other's bed.

Kara, now happily dating a man she'd grown serious about, had given her blessing a long time ago for Tania to hook up with Weldon. Still, she cautioned Tania about his wild, wicked ways. Yet, that was exactly why Tania liked him and the reason why Tania should stay away from him. Weldon was hot and a little too much to handle. Yet, she enjoyed *handling* him, thoroughly, during their private moments of bliss, away from the curious gawks of passerby.

Staying away from Weldon proved more and more difficult. Especially when his warm breath caressed her neck, ever so slowly, as he whispered near her ear that he wanted her. Sensing her affirmative response, he'd go a step further. He'd lick her skin or graze his blunt teeth along her softness until darts of pleasure warmed up parts of her that should've stood their ground and said *no*.

Damn it. Why did she always fall prey to him?

All she had to do was take one look into his irises filled with hunger and desire, and she gave in. It wasn't just the way he looked at her, though, like a starving man ready to devour a sumptuous meal, but the way he caressed and worshipped her body was an experience she never encountered with any of her lovers. Weldon was akin to a harpist stroking thoroughly over her strings, eliciting delicious moans from her mouth and delightful shivers through her body.

With Weldon, Tania was fresh out of conviction, except when dating him or something more serious. There was no way she was getting into that mess again.

Still, the more time she spent with him, the fonder she became. Weldon must've felt the same about her, for he drove her to his brother's inn one day and gave her a tour- an adventure he never shared with anyone before. They ended up having lunch there. That's where she saw Eva again. The beautiful, dark-haired female gazed upon them with a careful eye the entire time they were together.

Tania expected to continue meeting up with her regulars, but lately, she'd been slowing down. She spent so much of her time with Weldon it seemed there weren't extra hours for anyone else. Yet, she was fine with this as Weldon proved great company. He'd take her out on long rides through scenic landscapes in his Corvette or on rougher terrain on his motorcycle.

On occasion, her regulars asked her to go out, and she did. The visits, once blissful escapes, now turned into unusually awkward moments that were cut short, each time, by Weldon's phone calls or text messages.

Weldon knew she saw other men. Although he expressed his dislike regarding her dates on several occasions, for the most part, he kept quiet. She assumed he saw other women, as well, though the image of him lying naked in bed, intertwined with one or several other females, caused her to gag. Still, she had no say in the matter. There'd never been a conversation regarding their exclusivity.

Yet tonight was for her. She aimed to put her phone on silent as she accompanied one of her regulars, Lincoln, to a Halloween party with his friends. Lincoln was one of her favorites. A bad boy with a reputation, she always had fun in his company. Sometimes their meetings ended up with a bit of risky behavior, but she always had the option to opt-out. This was one of the things she liked about him. He never forced her to do anything.

Like Weldon, Lincoln had tattoos. Unlike Weldon, he had many strewn across his body and some in the oddest places. She likened his body to a curious maze, one where he occasionally added more rooms for her to investigate. She enjoyed those precious moments when he allowed her to explore his naked body, usually after a rough round of sex, to find his new ink. Lincoln wasn't the romantic type. No. That was more Joe or Miles. Sex with Lincoln was always raw and purposeful. When Tania had a particularly stressful day or just needed to feel wanted, she could always count on Lincoln.

Sex with Weldon was more meaningful. That's what scared her.

Although she was spending the night with Lincoln, she couldn't help but text Weldon a message to let him know she was thinking about him. Weldon knew she was out for the night. That didn't mean he wouldn't bother her, though. He always found some excuse to send a thoughtful message or some sort of reminder that he was still around. It amused her, but it also did something squirrely to her insides every time she received one of his messages. It meant he cared for her. His protective and jealous side strummed up something primitive within her and warmed through her. If she wanted Weldon, he'd come running. She knew it.

She wanted so badly to tell him he was the one for her. That she'd lay all her cards on the table and let him into her heart...Into her life, *permanently*. She wanted him to be the one, yet something was stopping her. Fear. That she might be right. That he might be the one she'd been waiting for. That if she gave herself completely to him, she'd eventually find him in bed with another woman. That would shatter her life completely. Her broken heart would be irreparable. All because she foolishly took a chance on a womanizer.

Lincoln's question interrupted her thoughts. "You ready, babe?"

The urge to run back home, jump into her car and find Weldon hit her hard. Why was she thinking of Weldon when she was supposed to have a fun night off, away from him? A ball of conflicting emotions welled up in the back of her throat, making it difficult for her to form a sentence, much fewer words. Did she want to go into the party, or did she want to fall back into Weldon's warm, loving arms?

Her heartbeats kicked up several beats as she glanced over at Lincoln. He was a handsome man. A little rough around the edges, his face tats might scare anyone, but they always fascinated her.

He grabbed her hand. The tone of his voice softened with his reassuring words. "Babe? We're going to have some fun."

Tania smiled back at him. She trusted Lincoln. She took his hand and followed him through the door and into a crowded, dim-lit room booming with music.

WELDON TOOK SEVERAL sips of his pumpkin-flavored coffee. One thing he liked about the holidays was the unique flavors attributed to this time of year. He looked forward to the small luxuries available. Taking full advantage of them until they slowly disappeared shortly after the New Year started.

He sighed, relishing the strong taste as his thoughts lingered on Tania. He'd love to share a cup or two with her if she were here right now, for she was a coffee lover, too. Instead, she was out tonight, at a party, with one of her *regulars*, as she called him.

Weldon snarled. The idea of the man, whoever he was, touching, caressing, or even kissing his mate tightened his muscles and had him gritting his teeth. He'd do anything to keep her safe.

At least, that was his excuse for the sudden surge of strong emotions creating a vortex within him. He had to protect her at all times. To let her go to some party with a man he didn't know was unheard of for his kind. However, he couldn't keep her caged at home like an animal. She needed the ability to roam free and make her own decisions even if some of those choices frustrated the hell out of him. The last thing he wanted was for her to end up in someone else's arms.

He had to applaud his recent efforts. He'd done a good job of reminding her he was still around when she wasn't with him. On those infrequent occasions, she dated one of the three men she had on the backburner. He waited till about an hour later and signaled her somehow by texting her or leaving a voicemail.

Sometimes he'd send her an emoji. She always liked those. Anything to let her know she was on his mind.

Holding back the urge to snatch and secure her within a vice grip, to prevent her from escaping to enjoy the night with one of her regulars, was becoming harder to do. Especially as he grew to know her. With the passing of each full moon's cycle, it was worse. He'd love nothing more than to grab her, throw her over his shoulder in a fireman's lift and carry her back to his bedroom. Like a caveman, he'd drag his delicious prize into his cave. Then he'd enjoy her fully and thoroughly under the powerful magnetic energy of the full moon, peeking through his slatted mini blinds into his private sanctuary.

Any excuse to keep her in his bed. She was safest when she was with him. Yeah. That was it.

Tonight, she was with another man.

His hands gripped the steering wheel as he strove to keep his attention on the road. Not particularly interested in staying home tonight when Tania was out having fun, Weldon took a last-minute delivery call and took off for the open road. Still, this one was only an hour away. He hesitated to accept any assignments requiring further distance between him and Tania. After all, if she needed him, he had to be available, just in case. She was his priority, after all, whether she knew it or not.

His fingers hesitated over her name in his contact list. It hadn't been an hour yet, and he never attempted to contact her earlier than one hour into her dates. If she was out with a girlfriend or even his ex, he didn't care. Yet, she was out with someone named Lincoln- that's all he was able to wrangle out of her. The name Lincoln conjured up too many images in Weldon's creative mind. What did he look like? What did he sound like? What was his personality? And most of all, what fascinated Tania about this guy?

What did Lincoln have that Weldon didn't?

The barrage of questions plagued his mind. Unanswered, they weighed heavily upon his heart. Sometimes he envied what his brother had. Eva was everything Kingsley waited for. A unique mate he'd never thought he'd find. While Kingsley never gave up, Weldon never dared to hope. Instead, he plundered available bedmates, searching for distraction and fun when he should've been waiting for Tania. He regretted his actions. If he was able to, he'd take it all back. For this was the one barrier between them, he could never erase. In hindsight, none of the females were worth his time or energy. Definitely not worth the crude nickname given to him or the mistrust of his mate.

Yet, each moment he spent with Tania, he spotted her marked desire and sensed her attraction to him. He also sensed her longing for something deeper with him. Still, his attempts to coax her into giving in met with staunch resistance. He knew she wanted more. Yet, the stubborn woman wouldn't change her mind about him.

For several long, blissful seconds, he thought he had her. He tasted victory, certain he convinced her to give them a chance. Yet, the next day, she sighed softly into the phone and whispered to him she was going out with one of her regulars that night. He pressed the phone to his heart as she ended the call.

The feeling of fullness and oneness he experienced in the presence of his mate was something that surprised him. It was an anomaly he couldn't begin to describe to anyone. Not enough for them to comprehend the complete satisfaction his heart and soul experienced when he was by her side. It was as if his two halves knew his search was over. Everything he wanted and needed, she possessed.

At a red light, minutes away from his drop-off point, he stared at her name on the screen. It had been more than an hour. He pressed her name, and the screen changed. Clicking on the microphone icon, he spoke his texted message to her while pressing his right foot down on the gas pedal as the red light switched to green. Then he ended the call, slipped the phone into his drink caddy, and waited.

TANIA GRABBED HER PHONE from her purse. She smiled as she glanced down at the screen.

Lincoln jutted his chin at the phone. "Need to take that?"

"Yeah. Give me a minute." She stepped off to one side. Weldon's words warmed through her heart.

Thinking about you. Let me know you're safe.

Thoughtful. That was another word she'd use to describe Weldon. He was always concerned about her well-being. It gave her warm, fuzzy feelings inside she hadn't experienced with another man in a very long time. Weldon truly cared about her. Although she was out with Lincoln, she couldn't help her feelings for Weldon. If he needed anything, she'd drop everything to be with him. It didn't matter. They weren't much more than friends. She cared about Weldon, too.

Her fingers flew over the keyboard as she texted her reply, ending her message with a red-lipped kiss emoji. Before she had the chance to add more, she pressed send and slipped her phone back into her pocket. She'd have fun tonight, but afterward, she needed to reconsider her relationship with Weldon. Maybe she'd sit down and have a chat with him. They couldn't go on as they were now.

Lincoln crooked his arm at her. "Join me at the bar?" She nodded. He skillfully maneuvered them through the crowd.

Smiles, laughter, and much conversation surrounded her. The upbeat music added to the atmosphere. Everywhere she went, it seemed people were having a good time. She knew no one and followed Lincoln's lead when he acknowledged a few at the party and introduced the host. The man's eyes shifted, and he, nervously, fidgeted and looked around. Yet, Lincoln didn't seem to notice. Instead, he swayed her toward the bar and ordered shots for them. He had just ordered another when the host slinked over to Lincoln's side and whispered something to him.

Lincoln turned toward her. "Hey, Gary wants to show me something, but it's downstairs. Come with me?" She took the hand he offered and followed him down a long length of stairs toward a hidden door she doubted anyone would find on their own.

"Where are we going?"

"There's a basement. He said whatever he has to show me is down there."

"But where's Gary?"

"He's coming. He'll be right behind us, he said."

She licked her dry lips. Her brows furrowed together in concern as she walked toward the large, etched door. Darkness swallowed them in with every step they took. Except for a few wall sconces, it was extremely hard to make out any details.

Lincoln tried the doorknob, and the door pushed in. He glanced back at Tania before taking several steps in. His left hand reached out toward the wall, searching for a light switch while his right hand held onto hers.

He pulled her further into the room. "There's got to be a switch in here somewhere."

Suddenly what little light was left disappeared. Tania's hand slipped out of Lincoln's. A high-pitched tone bellowed out of him, followed by a short groan. His body slumped onto something while Tania raised her hands out in front of her, attempting to pull off the scratchy material covering her head. She grappled at the ties, her fingers trying to make sense out of whatever crazy knots were used to secure the object surrounding her face. A mini eternity later, she moaned out her frustration. Something scampered across the floor and pinched her neck. She screamed. An icy cold substance was forced into her at the same time.

Her knees, suddenly, became wobbly. She slid toward the floor. Lincoln's name slurred out of her mouth, but there was no response. Something grabbed at her and hoisted her into the air. Her eyelids grew heavy. Her heart rate slowed. Her phone buzzed. Was it Weldon? All of a sudden, her hesitation to date him seemed silly. If she got out of this. If she escaped, whoever was doing this to her. If Lincoln was still alive —

She drew in one final breath of oxygen. Her jaw dropped with the last of her will and her eyelids closed.

Chapter Eleven

Weldon waited ten minutes. He picked up the phone, glancing at the screen like an eager kid on Christmas morning, anxious to find out if any gifts were awaiting him under the tree. Yet, there were no new messages for him. He waited another five minutes and checked again. Nothing. Tania always texted him back. It didn't matter who she was out with or what time of night Weldon contacted her, she responded. Yet, this time she didn't. It was unlike Tania. She knew how Weldon worried.

Was she ignoring him? Did she suddenly change their communication style without notifying him? Was she having *that much fun*, she forgot to reply? Weldon gritted his teeth. Yet, Tania wasn't that way.

Something was wrong.

He pulled the semi into a retail store parking lot, released the lock on the trailer, and lifted the door to reveal his motorcycle. Lowering the ramp, he climbed up it to reach his bike. After securing the trailer, he aimed toward home, traveling faster than possible with the empty semi. He couldn't waste any more time. He needed to locate her and fast.

"Call Eva." He spoke aloud and waited as his phone dialed. When she picked up, he immediately explained the situation.

He didn't know where Tania was, but he sensed she was in trouble. She had to be. She didn't respond.

At his current distance, he wasn't able to detect her whereabouts. Yet, once he got back in town, she was all *his*.

If Lincoln did anything to her—He'd soon learn who Weldon was and what happened when someone messed with his mate.

"If you find her, wait for me. Don't do anything without me."

"You don't want me to help her?"

He growled. "Lincoln is mine!"

"I think you're taking this too far. She's probably fine. She's out with someone she knows."

Weldon's tone of voice lowered two octaves. "No one truly *knows* anyone." He let the words linger in the air between them, the impact of their meaning settling in for several long seconds before he spoke again. "I mean it, Eva. Just monitor the situation and let me know if she is still alive." He received Eva's consent and then issued a warning. "Call me back." He ended the call.

To this day, Tania didn't know what he was. He attempted, at several times, to formulate some sort of foolproof plan, but, in the end, he came up with nothing. He wanted her to know him. To reveal his true identity in such a way she wouldn't run out his door screaming and vowing never to return. The risk of losing his mate was too great. Yet hiding who he was when he wanted to share himself entirely with her hurt him more than she'd ever know. Authenticity and honesty were paramount in any relationship. He could do neither with Tania.

Yet tonight, she'd find another side to him. One he never dared reveal before. If she ended up okay and unharmed, he'd still tell her. She deserved the truth. He couldn't hide what he was any longer. The question remained if she was strong enough to accept him.

TANIA'S EYELIDS SLOWLY lifted open and then, suddenly, shut closed. She grimaced, trying a second time to open her eyelids but this time ending in a faint squint. The blaring overhead lights had stunned her irises for a few seconds too long. She didn't want to repeat the error.

She slowly scanned her immediate surroundings. An empty floor with a semblance of metal rafters, now mostly disheveled, indicated that she was in some sort of abandoned warehouse. Spider webs hanging from parts of the metal confirmed the vacant part of her deduction. Yet, the building wasn't without life.

She lowered her head when she caught a low groan. Out of nowhere, she heard shuffling of feet, and then something slammed into a lump on the floor repeatedly. The whacks that dealt with the object were quick, violent, and excessive. She withheld a gasp as the groaning ceased. Then a door opened and shut.

She waited, desperate to find out if the object lying on the floor was still alive, but afraid someone fooled her, stayed behind, and was monitoring her actions. The light overhead proved to be only one instead of the several she expected to find. The brightness she experienced when she first opened her eyes was, in reality, dimmed. Whatever her captors injected into her must've still affected her. Blinking her eyes, she tried refocusing and then braced herself for the wave of imbalance and nausea slamming through her. She pitched forward, noticing for the first time her body immobile and her hands tied behind the back of a chair. Attempting to move her legs proved useless as well. Each one was bound to a chair leg.

She whispered to the object still lying on the floor. "Lincoln?" Yet, there was no way he'd respond, even if he was conscious. She moved her mouth to loosen the gag covering her lips, but the cloth barely moved. A dry lump formed in the back of her throat as she strained to make out who it was in the darkness. Did they kill him? Please no. —She made a high-pitched sound in the back of her throat before she realized she might've alerted her captors. Smart move. She'd kick herself if she could. Still, there was no response. The body on the ground didn't move.

The abject silence filled her with dread. If they killed him, what were they going to do to her?

Her head pounded as she moved it, attempting to strain her eyes to determine if it was Lincoln on the floor or if it was someone else. When she caught sight of blood by the body, her breath hitched. She had to find a way to get out of here and get Lincoln out, too.

Her focus returned to her restraints. She wiggled underneath them, squirming to find out how tightly bound they were when a light suddenly shone into the room through an open doorway. Bright, overhead lights burned her irises as a clicking sound hit her ears.

An upbeat tone accompanied a clean-shaven face. "Well, someone's awake."

She didn't recognize the man stepping in front of her, but she'd never forget his face. The nice-looking man had short, dark hair had impeccable taste in clothing, and sported chiseled features. If he didn't kidnap her, they might have had a beer or two and shared a good conversation.

He smiled as he leaned toward her. "Should we take that gag off now?" His companions surrounded the back of her chair. She counted them as they stepped up to her and ended at three. There were four total captors in the room. Whatever plan she came up with, she'd have to avoid all four of them in her escape.

The gag slipped off her, and she screamed for help. Mister Handsome laughed. "Scream all you want, little lady. No one's going to hear you." His chortle was mimicked by the others in the room.

"Who are you, and what do you want with me? With us?" She looked over at the lump on the floor. It had remained eerily still ever since.

Mister Handsome grinned. "You just happened to be in the wrong place at the wrong time. We don't want anything with you, but since we grabbed who we wanted, you're just a bonus." Mister Handsome turned his head toward the still figure on the floor. "He looks so peaceful, doesn't he?" Laughter filled the room.

Well, at least she knew the lump on the floor was a he.

"Did you grab my friend?"

Mr. Handsome's striking white teeth gleamed under the fluorescent lights. "Who? Lincoln? He's nobody's friend, girly. Don't you know that by now?"

Having received confirmation that the lump was now Lincoln, she turned to him, concern creasing lines into her forehead and causing a frown to her lips. "What did you do to him and why? Is he still alive? He did nothing to you."

Mister Handsome snickered. "You don't know him, do you? He was part of our gang once, but he decided we weren't good enough for him." One of the men approached the lifeless body and kicked it. He then spat at it.

"You're disgusting!" Her head snapped left with the hand slap she received in response to her observation.

"Be careful what you say. Next time might be worse." He looked her over. "Oh, we're going to have so much fun. Isn't that what Lincoln promised you?"

How in the hell did Mister Handsome know that? Were they watching him from the parking lot? She had to find out more information. Then she could plan her escape.

"Where am I? What are we doing here?"

"No more questions. You were at a Halloween party, and we sure like our parties. We love Halloween too. Lots of creatures of the night come out. All sorts of beings you'd never knew existed." She gritted her teeth and turned away when Mr. Handsome's fingers caressed her cheek.

"Get your hands off me." She swiveled toward him to bite his fingers, but he quickly moved his hand away.

He chuckled. "Oh no. We have a live one here, fellows. You like biting? So do we. In fact, Antonio fancies himself a vampire, don't you, boy?"

The man she figured was Antonio stepped up to her and smiled. She squinted her eyes to get a better look at his teeth when she thought she spotted something that shouldn't be there. Yup. There it was. Extra-long canines. Was he nuts? He tossed the gag to one of his teammates as she yelled a long line of expletives. The material slipped around her and tightened across her lips before she had the chance to further protest.

She squirmed and kicked out, trying to free herself from her binds. Her chair jostled and fell over with a bang. Tania's body vibrated with the impact to the ground. With little effort, Antonio and one other man righted her up again. Antonio's lips twitched. He moved closer. She screamed into her gag.

His hands, sporting calloused fingers, caressed over her, starting from random strands of her hair, down her cheek to her neck, and then latching, painfully, onto one breast. She wriggled with all her might to get away, but Antonio's pals just slid her chair up against a wall.

He whispered in her ear. She trembled with his dark declaration. "I like blood. You're going to give me a taste of yours before the night is through."

He slipped out a pocketknife and swung out the blade hidden within, holding it out in front of her eyes. The steel glistened like diamonds under the lights. She gasped when he flicked his tongue over the blade. Clearly, he was enjoying the fear she knew danced within her irises. He stalked toward her. Widening her eyes, she shook her head when he stood next to her, the steel blade by her arm. "I just want a little taste. Halloween's an excellent time of year to party. And that's what you came for? Right, sweetie? To party?" She cringed at the wicked gleam he gave her seconds before he sliced the blade into her upper arm. She screamed, the gag sabotaging her effort to convey her horror at her skin breaking open, blood streaming down her arm like a river.

His laughter was soon joined by the others in the room. "Vampires like to party." Antonio drew in a deep breath, an abnormally wide smile plastered across his face. He scooped up a line of red, dragging his index finger over her raw wound while she hissed through tight-sealed lips. He brought the drenched finger to his lips before plunging the liquid contents into his mouth. Closing his eyes, he rumbled his satisfied appraisal before opening his eyes and gracing her with another grin.

Her blood flooding through her veins, her heartbeat rapidly cycled through the panic and anxiety pumping the organ, urging her to find a way to get out and run. Tania glared up at him, hatred replacing her previous fear. She glanced across the floor to find Lincoln, yet the lump remained motionless. He was out of the picture and unable to help her. She had to do something. Yet, every means of protection she had available to her was either bound or covered up. Time was ticking, and their lives were on the line. What in the hell was she going to do?

Antonio lowered his head, maintaining eye contact with her the entire time while his tongue swept over her wet skin. She grimaced, squirming on her seat from him, as far away as possible. Her hands balled into fists with his uninvited intimacy while her fingernails dug into her skin. Antonio was soon joined by the others, all craving a taste of her liquid essence. A sick sensation rushed up the back of her throat and threatened to spew the last meal she ate into her gag. She gazed at the men, each taking turns licking her arm. One held up the knife, offering to cut another part of her for them to enjoy. As if on cue, they all stared at her right breast. She shouted at them and then screamed, the rumbling tone of her voice against the gag a stark reminder that they'd never hear her intended message. Not that it would make a difference. Instead, they delighted in the feast she unintentionally provided.

She wriggled and screamed again, her chair tipping over when Antonio suggested another idea. He intended to violate her while he ingested more of her blood. Then the rest would take turns. Oh God, no.

They all froze when a knock sounded at the door.

Antonio shouted to one of his cohorts. "Who in the hell is that? Get rid of him."

The guy stalked over to the door and opened it. He then placed the weight of his body against it and grunted as he attempted to shove it closed. The door banged inward off its hinges. Flew through the air to the opposite end of the warehouse, pinning the guy beneath it. Tania watched as the guy's body slid to the floor. Motionless, he remained while a rush of air blew through the opening and brushed back clumps of her hair, scattering the strands off her face. Suddenly a new man stood in front of Antonio. When he spoke, she knew exactly who he was.

Weldon sneered. His stern tone lowered in a warning. "You want to know what it's like to be a Vampire? I'll show you."

The next few seconds trapped her inside her worst nightmare.

Weldon, once standing in front of Antonio, suddenly was not. He magically evaporated into the air, showing up in front of each man only to vaporize into the atmosphere once more. Wails and cries erupted about the room, accompanied by cracking sounds. Blood spewed forth from the wounds Weldon created. Like mini waterfalls, the red color jetted out of them and stained across parts of Weldon.

She blinked her eyes, unwilling to recognize what was happening right in front of her. Yet, there was no dismissing the truth. Weldon whipped about the room at a rapid speed that couldn't be easily explained. Bodies crumpled to the unyielding floor, one by one as Weldon moved on to the next victim.

Tania shivered as a cold chill rippled through her. The warmth escaping her body wasn't solely due to Weldon's incredible descent upon the men who kicked up spurts of air that effectively lowered the temperature in the room. It was also likely due to the horrific images brambling about in Tania's brain as she attempted to figure out what Weldon truly was. He swarmed each of the men, roughly grabbing ahold of their necks and holding them still. Guttural cries filled her ears as Weldon's elongated incisors sliced into them like a knife through melted butter. Weldon seemed to enjoy the display of carnage. She trembled as a frosty shiver zipped up the length of her spine.

Weldon stopped and turned toward Antonio, making sure he had his attention before, intentionally, licking the spot of blood off the side of his mouth with a low growl. His facial features caught between a mixture of a grin and a jeer. He displayed his bloodied fangs before he dragged over the next to last victim, dropping him to his knees in front of a startled, wide-eyed Antonio. The man begged for his life, yet Weldon was un-phased, his entire focus on Antonio, who seemed too stunned to move.

"You want to know what it's like to drink blood." He turned toward the figure on the floor, frantically crying out in desperation and clawing at Weldon's tight grip on him. Weldon grinned as he shook him like a rag doll. Lust and a predatory craving she never knew existed danced through his unnaturally ice-colored irises. "You want to know the power of holding a person's life in your hands? I can end his useless existence, or I can let it continue. That is power. That is reality. You are all pawns in my game."

Weldon thrust the man's hand up in front of his lips. Inhaling a long, deep breath, he smiled as the man shouted his retort. He opened his jaw. His incisors lengthening, he latched onto the man's arm and dug in, sinking his teeth into the meat as if he was enjoying a delicious steak. His head bobbed slightly up and down as his mouth pulled from the man's veins. Weldon lifted up, his other hand squeezing into the man's neck, twisting it with little effort. A cracking sound ensued, followed by the man's body plummeting to the ground. He allowed Antonio to gape at him for several long seconds before he intentionally swiped his hand over the crimson red color streaming long rivulets from the corner of his mouth. He licked off the remnants with an extended, loud groan.

"Ahh. Delicious."

Antonio swiveled on his heel and ran, aiming for the door. Yet, Weldon was quicker. Less than two seconds later, Antonio stumbled into Weldon, already waiting for him.

Antonio held his hand out in front of him and backed up a few steps. "Please. Please don't hurt me."

Weldon threw his head back and cackled a spine-chilling tone Tania hoped never to hear again.

"You want me to spare you? You hurt the one woman who means everything to me."

Antonio glanced back at Tania. "Take her. It wasn't even my plan, to begin with. Please. She's yours."

Weldon's gaze met Tania's. She shook her head as she stared at the man she thought she once knew- the one whom she'd had sex with countless times. Something in Weldon's irises flickered. He thrust his hands in front of him, placing each on the side of Antonio's head. Antonio's head snapped to the right, and then his body fell to the ground.

Weldon strode quickly to Tania's side. She let out a loud squeal as he approached and squeaked several more protests into her gag while squirming in her seat as he drew closer.

He held a handout toward her. He caught her wide-eyed stare. "Please don't be afraid. I'd never hurt you."

Weldon swiveled to the back of her chair. Attempting to create distance between her and Weldon, she bucked in her seat and fell forward. He grabbed her, teetering her and the chair toward him, to stand with an unnaturally quick speed. Off-kilter and light-headed from the jostle, she waited till the room stopped spinning before she decided what to do next. If she thought the men were bad, Weldon seemed worse.

He untied the gag and threw it across the floor. Then, he kneeled in front of her, his fingers caressing over her arms until he found the wound. She jerked back from his touch. He closed his eyes and grimaced. "I know the last thing you want from me is a repeat of what those men did, but it is the only way to heal you. Will you let me lick you?" His gaze alighted upon her cut and focused back on her.

She stammered. Her body quivered. "What. Wh-at are you?"

He gripped her upper arms. She squealed. "Please. I won't hurt you. I'll never hurt you. Right now,, you are wounded. Let me heal you."

Unable to form words, she said nothing. Her mind raced with images as she tried to sort out everything that happened. This man, this-beast-pleaded with her to help her. He had just killed four men in front of her. Should she trust him? Did she dare trust the man she slept with several times in the past? She spent so many warm, cozy nights at his house, never knowing what he was capable of.

Tania's eyes flickered with the sensation of Weldon's warm, wet tongue across her skin. She shuddered when he was done. A sick sensation crawled up the back of her throat.

He cupped her chin and turned her to face him. "I'm sorry. I should've been here for you."

She swallowed the air, choking down as much as possible to fill her starved lungs. Then she dropped her gaze and whispered the startling fact rattling about in her brain. "You're not human."

Chapter Twelve

Gulping down the dry, uncomfortable sensation in the back of her throat, she tamped down the sudden urge to rip free of his grip. To flee. Knowing her running away wouldn't make the situation any better. The rapidly increasing tempo of her heartbeats due to his close proximity also did nothing to calm her. She resolved to remain strong and determined in her pursuit of information with the ultimate goal of making sense of the craziness she had just experienced.

Regardless of what happened, the last thing she wanted to do was display weakness in front of a beast that could rip her to shreds.

Despite the fact, she had once enjoyed Weldon's company, she would adamantly defend herself against him if she had to and die with dignity. Yet right now, she had to say something, tell him anything, to keep those piercing eyes off her. But, first, she had to gather her thoughts and her conflicting emotions. She had to place everything into perspective and attempt to make sense out of a senseless situation.

Her tone of voice was almost a whisper. "I saw what you did to those men. I heard what you said to them. You killed them, and you —" She drew in a shaky breath and then gave him a look of disgust. "Enjoyed it."

Whatever Weldon, essentially, was, he wasn't like her. She knew that now.

She'd enjoyed spending time with him and shared several secrets with him she shared with no one else. She grew to care for him, maybe even love him, and now —she wondered what in the hell he was and if what they had was ever real.

Weldon wasn't from Earth.

The incessant urge to bolt through the doors and escape far, far away from where he'd never find her clawed at her insides. All she wanted to do was shut out the vivid images flashing through her mind recalling every second that took place. It was like horrific photographs in a never-ending horror film reel.

Did anyone else know? Did Eva? If Kingsley was Weldon's brother, was he the same type of being as Weldon? What did Eva marry? Tania gasped.

She jerked her arms and feet out of the rope, previously binding her limbs together, and slid off the chair. Her legs wobbled. Still, she attempted to stand.

"No!" Weldon pulled her into his arms. "You've had an ordeal tonight. You need to rest."

She grimaced as she wriggled out of Weldon's embrace and then stilled when she peeked over his shoulder and found the lifeless lump still lying across the floor. Fear gave way to concern. She pointed at the object and pleaded with Weldon, her tone of voice wavering with her sense of dread. "Please. Help Lincoln. I don't know if he's —"

Weldon adjusted her in his arms to gaze into her eyes. "I'll get to him, but first, I'm worried about you."

She almost screamed, "But —he might not be alive!" before someone, from behind, grabbed her arms and gently unfolded her from Weldon's grasp. Tania pulled away from him, wide-eyed with her mouth agape. Swinging her head left to determine the face of her rescuer, Tania spotted familiar brown eyes gazing back at her.

"You'll be fine," Eva offered, assisting Tania toward the door while Weldon looked on. Tania glanced across her shoulder and found Weldon walking toward Lincoln's body. *Good.* At least Lincoln wouldn't be left behind.

Eva led her toward Lincoln's car, parked off to one side of the parking lot, but Tania jerked her hands up and broke free before they made it.

She took several steps back and cried out. "No! No! Stop it! Did you know what he was? Why didn't you tell me?"

Eva reached for her, but Tania scooted away. She shouted while the beginning of tears streamed from her eyes. "No! Stop. I won't go anywhere with you. You lied to me, and so did he. You could've told me the truth. I trusted you. I trusted him. Oh, God. It's all wrong." She hugged herself and then doubled over in an attempt to ease the queasy sensation rolling through her gut. When Eva took a step toward her, Tania shot a hand out in front of her, in a warning. "No. You've done enough. I want Lincoln, and I want to go home. I need to know if he's okay."

Just then, Weldon's form walked in her direction, carrying someone across his shoulders in a fireman's carry. Weldon spoke as he drew closer. "He is."

Tania started toward Lincoln, but Weldon held back. "He's unconscious, that's all. I'll take him home. You're not fit to drive. Eva will take you home."

Frustrated, dirty, and tired, Tania could take no more. She stamped her foot on the ground and shouted. "No! I'm tired of people telling me what to do. I'm not going with either of you. I want to go home with Lincoln."

Weldon gently propped Lincoln's body up in the backseat of Lincoln's car. He slipped Lincoln's keys out of his pocket and regarded them for a few long seconds before he replied. "Okay. I'll call Kara to pick you up, but I'm not leaving until Kara gets here."

"No. I don't want you around."

Tania quickly lowered her gaze. She regretted the impact of her words as soon as they were out. Regardless of what he was, he'd just saved her, and Lincoln's lives. Somewhere in the back of her mind, she knew she should be expressing her thanks instead of posing difficulties for him. Yet, Weldon had intentionally kept a secret from her, and so did Eva. A sudden, deep sadness mixed with betrayal swirled within her and threatened to overwhelm her heart. Why did stuff like this always seem to happen to her- granted, nothing involving other-worldly beings- that never happened. Yet, why did people always seem to end up breaking her heart? Especially when she dropped her protective barrier, let them in, and considered them friends?

Being stuck in close confinement with Eva or Weldon, when neither of them had the decency or the courtesy of opening up to her, was the last thing she wanted. Nothing Weldon said or did would erase the fact that he took advantage of her and acted human when he, apparently, wasn't. In all the months of dating, he had the opportunity to tell her, but he never divulged what he truly was. He also didn't give her a chance to make the big decision to be with him or not. Instead, he made it for her.

Still, the idea of Lincoln suffering any further because of her unwillingness to give in didn't sit well with her, either. Lincoln had been through enough tonight. He needed to be home, resting or possibly at the hospital, requiring medical attention. Yet, Weldon had the power to heal, right? She glanced at her arm but found no trace of where they cut her. Whatever Weldon did to her was amazing. Lincoln deserved to be healed, too, if Weldon was able to manage it. Yet, where Lincoln ached might end up too much of an endeavor for Weldon to pull off compared to her small cut.

"Can you heal Lincoln?"

Weldon nodded in response.

She delved further, hoping for a positive response. "Will you tell me what you are?"

"I can't, at your place."

Her eyebrows furrowed together. "You mean Kara doesn't know?"

"Very few know."

She pointed at Eva. "But she knows, right?"

There was a long silence before he replied. "Yes."

Tania slowly shook her head. "I can't believe you kept this from me."

"I'm sorry. I wasn't sure how to tell you."

Tania threw her arms up in the air. "You couldn't tell me? But, instead, you show up here as a —as a —vampire? Is that what you are?"

Weldon's gaze dropped. "I'm sorry."

Tania turned away from him and screamed out in frustration.

Weldon lowered his voice. "Let me take you and Lincoln home."

Bile built up at the back of her throat at the idea of sitting anywhere within Weldon's proximity. Still, she felt a tug in her heart, drawing her toward him and reminding her of the man she'd grown fond of, the man who warmed her bed many long, cold nights. The man who had just saved her from God knew what end-

Damn it. She should hear him out. She should give him a chance. Although he wasn't human.

Tania always had an interest, albeit more a morbid curiosity, regarding the paranormal. Yet, being faced with the possibility- in reality. —She wasn't sure if she wanted to know the truth or how she'd handle knowing everything about him.

Yet, Weldon rescued her and Lincoln when he didn't have to. He deserved to tell his story. To, at least, be heard.

Her hands visibly trembled as he took them in his. He softly tugged her toward him in an attempt to persuade her toward Lincoln's car. She looked up into his eyes, the corners of them crinkled with concern. Handsome as ever, Weldon, physically, looked the same as he did before. His sharp, defined features tugged at her heartstrings, urging her to forgive him for any indiscretion. Still, what she saw back there, in the warehouse- The blood. The violence. The rage. The vivid images lingered in her mind, keeping her nerves on edge and her senses and awareness on high alert. She shivered as she recalled what he did to the ringleader.

As if aware of her revulsion, Weldon whispered quietly, softly. "I'm sorry, Tania." He gently caressed the palms of his hands across her shoulders to soothe and minimize her discomfort. "I'm truly sorry that you had to learn about me this way. It wasn't what I intended."

Instinctively, she sucked in air and backed away, catching a swift glimpse of pain passing through his irises before he looked away and let her hands slip out of his. She grabbed his right hand before he had a chance to escape. He turned toward her, a glimmer of hope lighting up his irises and cracking further open his eyelids.

Fear grabbed ahold of her heart and squeezed it, sending a gasp rippling through her. Colorful images of Weldon callously snapping the necks of the humans, as if he were popping open bottles of soda, passed through her mind. She closed her eyes, willing the images to subside. Weldon wasn't like that. He only did it to protect her. That had to be the truth.

Tania gazed into a gorgeous sea of amber and green and pleaded, "Can you heal Lincoln now?"

He gently squeezed her hand. "It's better if he remains unconscious. He will remain so until I can get him back to his place. Then I can heal him properly."

She hesitated, needing to know the answer to her next question but unsure how to gently phrase it without hurting him. "How long have you been a vampire?"

Weldon slightly shook his head. "Let me explain in the car. We can talk along the way."

Tania dropped her shoulders in resignation. She opened the passenger door to Lincoln's car when she caught Eva and Weldon saying their goodbyes. Sliding into the passenger seat, she swallowed back a nasty retort when Weldon placed his hand atop her thigh.

He leaned over and looked her directly in the eyes. There was a mixture of sadness and something akin to regret darkening his irises. "Ask me anything. I want you completely comfortable with me."

Her gaze took in his fine features. His full eyebrows perched beneath smooth skin across his forehead were now etched with worry and concern, and his soft, chiseled cheekbones were partially tattooed in blood. He retracted his hand, which was spotted with the remnants of the angry red fluid of life that spilled from his victims. It was as if he was suddenly aware of how he must look to her. Weldon was a predator. He was a monster. Yet, the more she gazed upon him, the more she longed to forget everything she witnessed back in the warehouse. The more she longed to remember Weldon, only as the carefree womanizer with a motorcycle who pursued her. He was sexy back then—and—an amazing lover.

She mischievously grinned as images of Weldon holding her, pawing at her naked skin, and diving between her thighs to satisfy her flooded her memory. Yet, Weldon had fangs—Really long ones. Still, each time they had sex, he was gentle with her. She never knew he hid those monstrous things inside his mouth- twin objects that literally sucked the life out of everything it came in contact with.

Like a cat, spotted by a canary, Weldon stilled. His jaw tightened, and he swallowed hard with the horrified look she gave him.

He sat back in his seat and blew out a long, slow exhale. "I'm sorry, Tania." He then slid the key into the ignition and started the car.

AT LINCOLN'S PLACE, Tania looked on while Weldon "healed" Lincoln. At least that's what he said he was doing. Yet, when he sliced part of his wrist and fed it to Lincoln, Tania balked.

"Won't that turn him into a vampire?"

Weldon chuckled beneath his breath. He closed his eyes and sighed. A smile splayed across his lips as Lincoln pulled at his arm then grabbed the meaty length to fully indulge in the red liquid Weldon gave freely from himself.

Tania took two long steps toward Weldon and begged, attempting to pry Weldon's arm from Lincoln's determined grip. "Please don't."

"You don't understand." Weldon turned toward Lincoln as he opened his eyes. Centering himself in front of Lincoln, still in his clothes and on his bed, he locked their gazes then ordered Lincoln to forget what occurred in the past several hours. He filled in the blanks, instructing Lincoln to remember, only that he had an enjoyable night and that he took Tania home. Tania caught Weldon's quick glance at her and the smirk quirking up the corners of his mouth before he returned his attention to Lincoln with one final order. "Tania broke it off with you tonight. You'll delete her number and let her go so you can find another. It's for the best."

Tania sucked in air but held back from saying anything when Weldon stood and swung toward her. She mouthed,

"How could you?" to Weldon as he grabbed her arm and shuttled her toward the front door.

"We should leave him. He needs his rest. Besides, you broke up with him. It wouldn't look good if you remained here."

She squealed in protest as Weldon led her toward his motorcycle, parked in front of the building. He nodded once, acknowledging Eva as she disappeared into the trees.

Tania pointed at her departing form. "Doesn't she need a ride?"

Weldon smiled in response. He grabbed at Tania when she refused to take the helmet he held out to her. She took several steps back until Weldon stalked toward her.

She shook her head. "No. I don't want to go anywhere with you. Lincoln is healed, and I —I just want to go home."

He slipped a leg over his motorcycle. His amber, green eyes regarded her. "You don't want to know about me?" Then he reached for her, wiggling the tips of his fingers in a gesture of come-hither as he cocked his head to one side with a smooth smile splayed across his lips.

Damn. Despite being some strange version of a blood-sucking animal, the man was gorgeous. Or- maybe it was because he was a vampire that she, and seemingly every other woman that existed, was drawn to him and his sexual prowess. As badly as she wanted her legs to run, they stayed bolted to the ground. He called her name in that sexy, low tone of voice that always had her ending up in his bed, between the sheets, or in some other sordid act of submission. *Lord*. When it came to Weldon, she was a goner.

TANIA RECALLED THAT night, a little more than two weeks ago, when Weldon answered all her questions. Since then, Tania tried to forget what she saw that night and pretend that he was just your average joe human, yet the nightmares had only begun.

As if sensing she needed him, Weldon called her cellphone countless times and even came over, unannounced, once. She hadn't told Kara what he was. Who would believe her, anyway? She was thankful she'd gone out the night he swung by for a surprise visit to sit alone in a restaurant rather than face irresistible, handsome Weldon at her door. That was a feat better suited to his ex, who now had a steady boyfriend.

The fact that Weldon was turned by a one-nightstand didn't sit well with her, either. Yet, she had no power to change the past. If she did, she'd end his vampire and turn him back into a wolf shifter again, for that's what he, essentially, was.

Of course, she wasn't prepared to find out that he was anything other than human. Witnessing his vampire skills was enough, but to find out he had another beast within him? She slid to the edge of the sofa when his wolf senses had him pouncing toward her. Damn, the man was fast when he wanted to be. Unfortunately, she was scared out of her mind.

When he toppled them over and onto the floor and gazed at her with kind, beautiful eyes, she found her body betraying her. It, easily, melted into his as if they were made for each other.

He whispered, hotly, by her earlobe. "I love you, Tania. I have since I met you. Please don't fear me. Please don't ever be afraid of what I am. I would never hurt you. I swear on my life, I wouldn't."

That's when he folded her within his strong, powerful arms and kissed her. She softened within his embrace and let him do everything to her that gave her joy. Yet, she wasn't prepared for the scrape of his teeth against her throat.

Chapter Thirteen

Opening her eyes, Tania muffled a scream when she found Weldon towering over her, his fangs extended in his open mouth. He closed his lips quickly, but he couldn't hide the one extra-long fang slipping past the edge of his upper lip. She traced the outline of it with her index finger. He retracted it before she had the chance to continue marveling at it.

She caressed her fingers down the side of his cheek. "You'd never harm me? Even if I upset you?"

He shook his head. "No, Tania." He placed her hand across the left side of his chest. "You are here. I can never hurt what is a part of me."

"Does anyone else know?

"Only Eva. That's why it gladdens me that you, too, know. Not even my brother knows. But I'm happy that you, the one who is dearest to me, now knows." He nuzzled behind her ear, forcing a sweet, satisfying moan from her lips.

"Tania. You undo me. You are like the sweetest, richest wine I've ever tasted. I simply have to have more."

Between his loving caresses, she whispered his name, her insides swirling with a pleasurable mix of sparking electricity and feel-good chemistry.

"Sixty years I've been a vampire. I've never regretted it until tonight when you looked at me the way you did back at the warehouse."

She gasped. "Did you say-sixty-oh- oh my. How old are you?"

"Age is just a number, sweetheart." His grin fell with the alarmed look on her face. "Don't be scared. I'm not that old. Only about one hundred and eighty-five, human years, that is, but who's counting?"

"Oh, my- God."

He smirked. " God had nothing to do with what I am."

"You look like you're in your thirties."

He winked. "Why, thank you."

She placed her hands on his chest and gently pushed him away so she could look up at him. "No, Weldon. I'm serious. You've lived that long, and you've seen so much. What do you want with me?"

He brushed his lips against hers. "Darling, I've lived a while, yes, but in all my years of life, I've never found anyone as delightful as you."

"Truly?"

"Truly. Now open that sweet mouth of yours."

A shiver ran through her as she closed her eyes, recalling what happened next. Her bad boy, now half-vampire, half-wolf shifter, swept her up into his big, brawny arms, eased her back onto her feet in his spacious shower, and then lathered her up in more ways than one.

She shook her head as she recalled every delicious detail of their lovemaking. Weldon backed her up to a wall and then roughly took her. His hands gripping the sides of her hips, she wrapped her legs around his waist as he powered into her. He finished off her orgasm with a shallow bite to her bare shoulder. She flinched at first, but then curiosity grabbed ahold of her, and she urged him deeper. He pierced his lengthening fangs through her skin- the dual feeling of him elsewhere, within her, inexplicably erotic. When he slowly siphoned her Type A positive essence, she threw her head back and uttered a loud, long moan while her sensitive nipples hardened into rigid, platinum grade strength pebbles.

After what seemed several long, sweet, satisfying minutes, he licked the wound, rested his cheek against hers with a low sigh, and pulled back enough to gaze directly into her eyes. "You are the most gorgeous woman in the world, to me. Thank you for accepting me, as I am."

Tania didn't know what to think. She'd just had even better sex with the one man who made her feel all sorts of emotions she never felt with anyone else before. Yet the way he held her, gazed at her, and spoke to her, she automatically knew what they just engaged in meant more to him than pure sex.

Weldon genuinely cared about her.

At times, the way he held and caressed her reminded her of how a person holding a precious, delicate object would act.

Weldon made it clear he wanted her. Yet, if she wanted him, there was their future to consider.

He tossed her onto the bed and lay down beside her. She fingered his tousled locks of hair while silently marveling at his aesthetic perfection. "Will you live forever?"

He chortled. "Yeah, I guess. Unless someone takes my head off."

"Are there any others like you?"

"Not sure, but I imagine so. I haven't encountered any more since my turning."

She grimaced as an unwelcomed image popped into her head. A deep sadness accompanied a dull pain in the pit of her stomach. "But —aren't there any females like you that you can be with? I mean, forever is a long time." She shied away with her last few words. "Humans die."

A short silence ensued. He looked her over, slowly, as if, carefully, considering her words. Then he shrugged his shoulders. "If there were, I wouldn't be interested. I've already found my one."

"But-Weldon, I—" She glanced away, unwilling to cause him further pain by uttering words he likely wouldn't want to hear. She loved being human. She had no interest in being anything but-

His gentle voice pinged across her eardrums. "I understand. You don't want to become like me. I want you, Tania, but not under any duress. I want you, as you are, for your entire lifetime. That is enough for me."

She sighed the slight tension surrounding her heart, relaxing with the earnest tone of his voice. Weldon truly cared about her. He wasn't going to force onto her what was given, unwillingly, to him.

"Thank you, Weldon."

He leaned toward her and gently caressed his fingers down the side of her cheek as he caught her gaze within his. "The question is—will you accept me?"

"I want to. You rescued me and—"

He shook his head. "I don't want you indebted to me. You are my mate. I will always rescue you. That is one thing you must understand." He paused, drawing in a deep breath of air before continuing. "Understand, too, that I don't want you to accept me because you have to. I want you to accept me because you want to." He cupped her chin, forcing her to gaze directly into his eyes. "I want you, Tania. Only you. If you're not ready for me, I will wait for you until you are."

After pouring her a glass of water and leaving her side, Tania slipped out his front door and into an Uber while he took a shower. She regretted it now.

There was nothing she could do at the time. It was too much information to take in at once, and she needed time to process everything. Weldon couldn't expect her to joyfully commit to him without thinking things over, could he?

Never the type to leave a stone unturned, especially when it came to her knowledge of him, she scrolled up to the text message where Weldon informed her there was a way of turning humans. The reason why he brought up the subject, at all, was because of her. She'd asked if what he did to Lincoln would turn him, and he had said no. He then offered that there was a way to do so and that he had never turned anyone. He had never had an interest, before, in doing so. Still, if the intention to turn a human was there and if the vampire willed it during the healing process, the human could turn. If she wanted to become like him, he would try with her one day- just for her.

Weldon offered it as an alternative to her dying. She didn't think she'd take him up on that offer anytime soon. Yet, it was good to know.

Tania's main concern forming a commitment to Weldon was that she'd, eventually, pass away and leave Weldon bereft of a partner, to wander the Earth alone for the rest of his life. Now she knew there was another option. Still, the idea of her becoming anything besides herself had her stomach turning and bile sliding up the back of her throat. Maybe, if she was desperate enough or on her death bed, she might consider it. Not now. She hadn't made up her mind, yet, whether to spend forever with him or not.

If she made that commitment to him, she'd be loath to change her mind. Leaving him after making such a grand decision would be unpardonable. One would have to be cruel, heartless, or unfeeling to lightheartedly toss a decision out and then retract it, especially when Weldon informed her she was the only option for him.

Yet here she was, saddened and behind the counter, again, at Shenanigans. The only difference, this time, was that Eva was making her way up to her.

Eva took a barstool and leaned forward, resting her arms across the countertop. "He misses you, you know."

Tania thrust her hands out to her sides. "Why are you here? You can get a beer anywhere."

"I just want to talk. Don't be mad at me. It's really up to him to tell you what he is. Not me."

Tania swallowed back a dry lump in her throat. Eva was right. The decision to disclose what Weldon was laid with him and no one else.

Still, Tania wasn't ready to make friends with Eva yet.

Tania called to a petite young woman with long, brown hair to her right. "Chichi, can you take care of this customer?" Tania turned toward Eva. "I've got to go." She dropped her bar towel onto the counter and walked away.

"Call him. I've never seen him so —so —sad and miserable."

Eva's words sliced a knife through her heart. Weldon. Sad and miserable? *Nah.* More like cocky and over-confidant. That was everyday life for Weldon. Yet, when Eva used those words, a humbling, grey image appeared in Tania's mind. Weldon, sitting in his easy chair, with a marked frown and slumped shoulders, gazing at his phone, anticipating a call or text message from Tania that never came. The image disturbed Tania. Was Weldon truly melancholy and heartbroken?

Tania couldn't let that happen.

She slipped her cellphone out of her pocket on the way out the side door of the building to call him on her break when she spotted a familiar form by an unmistakable, brightly colored vehicle.

With his arms folded across his chest, he leaned back against the car and smiled at her.

"Weldon? What are you doing here?"

He pulled down his dark glasses and winked at her. "Nice to see you too, Tania."

She shook her head. "But-what- are you following me? Ohhh —I get it. Eva called you and told you I was working today."

"No." He paused a short while and regarded her with a mischievous grin. "You mean, you haven't seen me? Boy, I'm better than I thought."

"What? What are you talking about?"

"I've been keeping an eye on you for the last two weeks." He pushed off the Vette and took a step toward her. "You see,

Tania, regardless of if you call me or not, I will always protect you. You're too precious for me to lose."

She stared at him, her mouth opening and then closing, unable to form words. What he confessed to her was incredible. He stayed near her, beyond her notice, to protect her. Who did that?

She shook her head. "I-I- don't know what to say except thank you."

He trudged up to her in his heavy boots, his towering form shadowing hers in the dimming light. A ring of hope tinged his irises. "Tell me that you're mine. That's all I want to hear."

She whispered his name but said nothing further. How could she make a split-second decision that would affect the rest of her life? The past few weeks, she'd been trying to forget about him and move on. A task she found not so easy, in the end.

Weldon slumped down his shoulders. His strong physical form changed into a meek shadow of a man. "You don't care for me. I should've known the one woman meant for me wouldn't want me in the end." He turned to walk away.

Her heart filled with trepidation. A gnawing sensation urged her mouth to open and call him back to her. Instead, she mindlessly watched him as he trekked back to his car.

He glanced back at her once before opening the car door. Her heart jolted in her chest. He was leaving her. *Nooo.* What did she do?

She reached for him, her hand stilling in front of her in the cold night air. "Weldon!" She gulped in a short breath of air when he swiveled toward her. "Please. —Please just give me some time."

He nodded once, slipped into the driver's seat of the car, and then sped away.

DAMN IT. What in the hell was wrong with her? Spending her lifetime with a half shifter, half-vampire? It couldn't be all that bad, could it?

Still, saying *yes* to him was scary.

A vivid image of solid metal bars, sliding down all around her from somewhere up above, locking into place and effectively imprisoning her, kept her mouth from forming the words he wanted to hear. Would the word *yes* lead to her demise or to newfound freedom she'd never known before?

Since the nightmarish day when Weldon drove off, they spent every night since talking for hours on their cellphones. She enjoyed their chats that often extended into the wee morning hours of the next day. It was as if they just met and were starting to get to know each other. Eventually, Weldon came over. Somewhere in the month he courted her, she forgave Eva. When Weldon brought Tania to his brother's inn, her heart warmed at the fact that he cared enough to show her his world. Yet, when Weldon escorted her into Kingsley's home, a cozy, comfortable log cabin in the middle of nowhere, Tania's heart set aflame at the notion that Weldon wanted more. She laughed as images of Weldon flew in and out of her brain. He was the most frustrating man, selfish at times but truly considerate of others when he wanted to be. And now—he was knocking at her door.

Weldon held the gorgeous bouquet of flowers out in front of him. An arrangement of vivid, complementary colors, the various array of flowers caused the corners of her lips to curve up into a grin. She snatched it from him, drawing him into a tight, appreciative hug afterward.

"Thank you so much, Weldon." She indicated the living room with one wave of her hand. "Please come in."

He crossed the threshold and sat on one of the barstools lining the front of the granite stone countertop. She caught his warm smile as he watched her arrange the flowers into a large, crystal vase. Once she was done, she joined him on the barstool next to him.

She grabbed ahold of his hands in hers. Rubbing her thumbs across the back of his hands, she stared at the floor as she attempted to formulate sentences. This was her chance, her shining moment, to speak the words that were screaming from inside her. The confusing blur of sentences she hesitated to form before, due to an uncertain future with him, blocked the life-giving air in her throat, and she found herself choking instead.

Weldon leaned toward her. He furrowed his eyebrows in concern. "You okay? Why is your heart rate so rapid?'

She forgot the vampire side of him, able to engage her vitals faster than any nurse could.

She slowly nodded, giving his hands a slight squeeze, in thanks, before looking into his eyes. "I love your world, Weldon."

His lips parted. Golden flecks sparkled in his eyes. "What are you trying to say to me? Do you agree to be a part of it?"

She gave him a shy smile. "I would like to." He pulled her off the stool and brushed her into his arms before she could further speak.

She nudged her hands against his chest. "Wait. There's something else I have to say."

"Speak, my love, for there is nothing you could possibly say to tarnish this moment."

She giggled. "I love you. No, wait-" He snatched her up into his arms and raced for her bedroom.

"No, Weldon. You're not giving me a chance to speak."

He laid her across her soft comforter, taking care to gently place her head onto her pillow. Then he straddled her on the bed and gazed straight into her eyes. "You have more to say? Tell me everything you need to so that I can enjoy you and the start of our new relationship together."

She caressed the back of her hand down the side of his cheek. "It's just that I'm scared, Weldon, but I do want to be with you, and I know you'll take care of me just as I'll take care of you."

"That is all that matters, my love. You and I."

She whispered to him as he nudged away wisps of her hair, hiding her bare neck to him. "No more secrets?"

He grazed his blunt teeth against her sensitive skin. "None."

"Good. I'm yours, Weldon."

"As I am eternally yours."

Tania gasped, her heart flooding to capacity with joy, as Weldon's fangs punctured through her warm skin and siphoned her essence, sealing, forever, her fate with his.

The End

Also, By TK Lawyer

(The Guardian League)
Jasper
Centurion
Apollo
Aeron
Orion
Stand-Alone Novels
Angels and Diamonds
Shifter Shorts
Serenade
Crossroads
Her Other Guardian
Nightfall
Anthologies
Love on the Edge of Danger:
A Pandemic Romance Collection
No Man Left Behind

About

Passionate * Playful * Paranormal

INTERNATIONAL BESTSELLING Author, Tamara K. Lawyer, writes under the pseudonym TK Lawyer and was born in Colon, Panama. She moved to the United States with her family to pursue her post-secondary education aspirations and found her love of writing shortly after.

She writes sexy, heartwarming, paranormal, and contemporary romances. Her books often toe the line, straying from traditional ideas to open reader's minds and hearts to unlimited possibilities.

When she isn't reading or writing, she is likely spending time with her husband/best friend or catering to their lovable American Foxhound, Misfit, who steals all the attention in their house.

Connect with TK

Amazon[1] Facebook [2]Twitter [3]Website[4]

Don't miss out!

Visit the website below and you can sign up to receive emails whenever TK Lawyer publishes a new book. There's no charge and no obligation.

https://books2read.com/r/B-A-SZJD-NPTQB

BOOKS 2 READ

Connecting independent readers to independent writers.